"Want to arm wrestle?" Dusty challenged.

Miguel took his eyes off the road to glance at her. "You must know I'm stronger than you are. Why do you always want to deny the difference between our sexes? What are you afraid of, little lady?"

Dusty bristled. "I'm neither *little* nor a *lady*. I just think I could beat you."

"Okay then, you're on. But there should be a prize." His dark eyes danced with mischief. "How about a kiss?"

Dusty squirmed in her seat. "On the cheek?"

Miguel stopped the truck and turned to face her. "I was thinking more of a long... slow... wet... meeting of the mouths."

"Oh." Dusty's eyes focused on his full lips.

Miguel leaned closer. "What prize will you claim?" His warm breath ignited a fire within her that threatened to flare out of control.

"The same," she answered breathlessly.

"An author to watch for," said *Romantic Times* magazine of Sharon Mayne's first Temptation novel, *Heart Trouble*. In her second book, she has created a heroine who braves the back country of Arizona and Utah alone, but shies away from men until she meets one with all the right moves. A resident of Arizona, Sharon loves to explore the wilderness with her husband and two Airedales. Watch for her third wonderful Temptation story featuring a hunk of a hero named Steele Erickson—available in March 1993.

Books by Sharon Mayne

HARLEQUIN TEMPTATION
390—HEART TROUBLE

THE RIGHT MOVES

SHARON MAYNE

Harlequin Books

TORONTO • NEW YORK • LONDON
AMSTERDAM • PARIS • SYDNEY • HAMBURG
STOCKHOLM • ATHENS • TOKYO • MILAN
MADRID • WARSAW • BUDAPEST • AUCKLAND

To Joan Elliott Pickart and Thomas Robert Moehn,
again and always

Published November 1992

ISBN 0-373-25519-5

THE RIGHT MOVES

1

"A Slow, Comfortable Screw against the Wall."

To Dusty Rose, the words echoed through the restaurant, rising above the strumming of a Spanish guitar and hushing the conversation of the other diners. She forced her hand to scrawl an abbreviated version of the order. After four winters of waiting tables at various ski resorts throughout the West, she'd thought she'd heard them all: Fuzzy Navel, Hairy Navel, Dirty Mother, Skip and Go Naked, Sex on the Beach, Screaming Orgasm....

But a Slow, Comfortable...?

She cleared her throat. "What exactly goes in that?" she asked the table of college boys celebrating a cohort's twenty-first birthday. She kept her expression calm and professional, pretending she didn't see them elbow one another or hear their snickers.

At twenty-five, she felt neither embarrassed nor intimidated by the younger men's leers. But the thought of ordering the drink from Miguel . . . She bit her lip to keep from moaning aloud.

Miguel Santiago. Bartender and son of the restaurant's owner. He was close to thirty with sable-brown eyes, glossy black hair, dusky skin and a voice like honey. A man, not a boy.

When they'd been introduced, he'd taken her hand in both of his and raised it to his lips to kiss. Dusty had instantly pegged him as the resident Romeo, the guy who always tried to be the first to bed the new girl.

Through the past two days of her training, his warm gaze had followed her every move, but, unlike the other Restaurant Romeos she'd met, he'd made no overt pass she could reject and be done with it. Instead he'd tried to charm her with old-world gallantry.

How could she object when he opened doors or pulled out her chair? Paid her extravagant compliments? Offered to carry her heavy trays?

She couldn't afford to be rude to him. She needed a job, and Pinecreek, Arizona was no ski resort with bars and restaurants a dime a dozen. Here in the mountains, two hours north of Phoenix, business dwindled in the autumn and winter. She'd arrived in early September and quickly discovered that most restaurants were laying off, not hiring.

And now this had to happen, she fumed, on her first night on her own.

One of the guys answered her question. "Slow as in sloe gin." Dusty snapped out of her reverie and scribbled as the others added their explanations.

"Comfortable as in Southern Comfort."

"Screw means orange juice, as in a Screwdriver."

"Against the Wall means Galliano, as in a Harvey Wallbanger."

Dusty nodded curtly and glanced at her order form. Two Mexican beers, two margaritas and . . . that one. So much for drinks. "Anything else? The blue corn nachos with bay shrimp make an excellent appetizer."

"Just another bowl of chips and salsa," the birthday boy answered.

Dusty nodded again, not surprised that the group would limit itself to the freebies. Although small, La Margarita was no cheap hole-in-the-wall Mexican restaurant. The selection of entrées extended far beyond the usual tacos and enchiladas. White linen and crystal candle globes decked the tables; plush, burgundy carpeting stretched across the floor; heavy wooden beams lined the walls and plastered ceiling, and oil paintings decorated the spacious room.

She launched into her sales pitch, although she figured the group would aim for the lower-priced meals to save their money for drinks.

"For dinner, the chef is recommending the *huachinango Veracruz*. That's fresh red snapper baked with lemons, tomatoes, green chilies, sweet peppers, garlic and onions." She paused for breath, then continued. "The shrimp margarita is—"

"We'll think about dinner after we've had our drinks," one of the guys interrupted and Dusty reluctantly turned toward the bar.

At least Miguel was alone, she thought. No customers sat at the bar to hear her order *that* drink. Gritting her teeth, she fixed a neutral expression on her face and forced her unwilling feet forward. Miguel greeted her with a grin, his teeth white and even against his olive skin. She tore the order form off the pad and offered it without speaking, but he made no move to take it.

"Just call it out like Luisa trained you." His dark eyes gently encouraged her.

She opened her mouth, then snapped it shut when she realized that she usually prefaced her orders with, "I need a . . ." No way was she going to tell Miguel she needed a Slow, Comfortable Screw against the Wall.

"Two margaritas," she said instead, "a Tecate, a Dos Equis and . . ." She mumbled the last drink while Miguel dropped ice into a blender, then added lime juice, tequila and triple sec.

Sighing with relief, she figured he was familiar with the drink and wasn't going to tease her. She ran a lime around the edges of the goblets and dipped them in salt. Miguel pulled the two beers from the refrigerated section behind him.

As she stuck wedges of lime into the top of each beer bottle and set them on a tray, he poured the margaritas and asked, "What was the last one?"

Dusty stared at the knot of the black tie topping his white tuxedo shirt. He hadn't understood her mumble. She was going to have to repeat it.

Just look him in the eye, she commanded herself. *Call out the order and give him the deep freeze. You know how to put a Restaurant Romeo in his place.*

Her gaze dropped lower, following the trail of his tie down his wide chest. She couldn't do it. Something about Miguel tugged a reluctant response from her and that flustered her.

He probably wore a gold chain, she thought scornfully. He simply wasn't her type. Why was she letting him intimidate her? And why could she so easily picture that gold chain gleaming against his dusky skin?

Her gaze, still descending, hit the red satin of the cummerbund spanning his narrow waist and she gathered her wits before her wayward imagination went into overdrive.

"Sloe gin, Southern Comfort, orange juice and Galliano," she answered.

"That's a Slow, Comfortable..." There was anger in his voice. "Are those guys giving you trouble?" He scowled across the room at the college boys.

Too startled to answer, she stared at him. His dark eyes focused on her, fiercely protective.

"If they are, just say so. I'll throw them out." He moved to the end of the bar and lifted the hinged section as if to exit.

"No, they're just kids," Dusty said quickly, finding her voice. In her experience, restaurant owners didn't care how customers treated their waitresses as long as they paid their bill. "I carded them. They're okay."

"I know you carded them. I gave you the register for them to sign." He moved back to the serving well, placed his hands flat upon the bar and leaned toward her. "The question isn't if they're old enough to drink. The question is, are they harassing you?" His square jaw was locked, giving his face a stern expression.

"No," Dusty answered in the same firm tone. "I can handle them." *You're the one who throws me off kilter,* she complained silently, returning his gaze.

Apparently satisfied with what he saw, Miguel mixed the drink. Dusty continued to fume. The last thing she needed was another charming and undependable man in her life. She already had one. In fact, she'd come to Pinecreek to find him. Once she got her hands on him, she wasn't sure if she'd kiss or kill him, but the longer the search took, the longer the list of her grievances grew.

Miguel happened to top that list at the moment, but the girlie-girl clothes waitresses were required to wear at La Margarita ran a close second. The ruffled hem of the skirt made her legs itch—or was that from the constriction of the despised panty hose? The lace on the scooped neckline of the peasant-style blouse chafed her skin and the elastic edge of the puffy sleeves cut into her biceps.

She far preferred the black slacks, white oxford shirt and bow tie she wore to wait on tables at ski resorts—where she also made more money, another item high on her list. Pinecreek was a retirement town, and the senior citizens who comprised most of La Margarita's clientele seemed to think the ten percent tip of their youth still adequate.

Miguel broke into her thoughts as he set the drink upon her tray. "You don't have to take any guff here. This is a family business and we don't tolerate rudeness from our customers any more than we do from our employees. Got it?"

"I can handle them," she repeated, picking up her tray. She'd been fighting her own battles all her life and felt a trace of resentment that he should question her ability. But his protective attitude was also the opposite of what she'd expected and for that she was grateful.

"Thank you, anyway," she added and walked away, feeling more confused about Miguel than ever.

MIGUEL WATCHED HER LEAVE, balancing the small round tray full of drinks with ease. He couldn't seem to keep his eyes off her; already his sisters had noticed and begun their merciless teasing. But he couldn't stop himself.

Born and raised in the restaurant business, he'd been a people watcher for as long as he could remember. Body language, he believed, revealed more about a person than words. But he couldn't read Dusty Rose. Barely three inches shorter than his own six feet, she towered over his petite sisters, yet didn't slump to minimize her height. She moved with an unconscious, feminine grace and a slight sway to her hips that swirled the ruffle of her black work skirt around her shapely calves.

The embroidered apron with its pink sash accentuated her slim waist and the flare of her hips. The white peasant-style blouse covered a nicely rounded swell of breast at the same time its puffed sleeves revealed a definite curve to her biceps. Muscles she'd developed, he assumed from reading her application, when she worked as a ski instructor as well as a waitress. In the warmer months, she conducted four-wheel-drive tours through Canyonlands National Park near Moab in Utah. Her hobbies were backpacking, river running and rock climbing. Fragile, she wasn't.

But her features were delicate: big brown eyes fringed with long, dark lashes, a pert nose, high cheekbones, an enticingly full lower lip. Her honey-blond hair was long, halfway to her waist, even when pulled back into a braid.

Her hair emphasized her femininity, yet she chose not to adorn it or to use cosmetics to enhance her lovely facial features. Neither did she wear jewelry. And the shoes she chose to wear with her work skirt were thick-soled, obviously comfortable . . . and hideous. When she caught him admiring her, her expression grew cold and she glanced away, but not before he saw a hint of shyness in those big eyes.

He sensed something else about this strong, capable, forthright woman, something untouched . . . even virginal. That, he knew, was highly unlikely at her age, especially considering her life-style, but he'd bet dollars to doughnuts that she had never experienced passion in a man's arms.

He'd like to be the one to teach her. He grinned as he absently polished the bar, imagining her as a luscious dessert: her hair like spun taffy, her eyes like melted milk chocolate and her skin a golden caramel. Yes, he could feast on her, all right.

"Daydreaming, Miguel?" his sister, Ramona, interrupted. "Or did you make a date with Dusty?"

"I don't date people I work with, Mona," he retorted, handing the small brunette her packet of tickets. "And you're late. You were supposed to be here at five, not quarter after. Dusty has her hands full with a bunch of college punks and four other tables."

"I told Mamá I'd be late, and you didn't answer my question." Ramona's dark eyes twinkled as she looked at him. "Mamá wants grandchildren so badly, I don't think she'd mind a tomboy like Dusty for a daughter-in-law."

"Carmen's already given her two and now Luisa has one on the way. Get to work and help Dusty. Luisa's seating another table."

"But only *your* children will be Santiagos."

"Which means that Mamá will want their mother to be Mexican." Miguel returned his sister's smug grin, certain he'd had the last word, but she shook her head.

"She's so worried you'll never settle down, she wouldn't care if your wife were purple as long as she had your babies!"

Miguel laughed, but refused to be outdone. "And why is a good Mexican girl like you going to college instead of getting married and having children?" Ramona stuck out her tongue at him and flounced into the dining room.

Miguel could see the welcoming smile Dusty gave his youngest sister. He wished she'd smile at him that way. There was no rule about dating employees. Besides, she'd return to Moab in the spring. What harm could there be in getting to know her a little better in the meantime?

Easier said than done, he realized when the restaurant closed and he offered her a drink. She refused until his sister added her entreaties. Then the two of them plunked down onto bar stools, accepted the white wine he poured and proceeded to treat him as if he were invisible.

A senior at Pinecreek College and an environmental science major, Ramona plied Dusty with questions about her job in Canyonlands Miguel eavesdropped shamelessly while he restocked the bar and took inventory.

"As a tour guide, you have to be a little of everything," Dusty was explaining. "Medic, entertainer, chef, historian and geographer. That you can get the jeep over hill and dale, the customers take for granted." She chuckled.

"It's dangerous, isn't it?" Miguel asked.

"The slickrock can be tricky," she answered, then turned to Ramona and lowered her voice. "But not nearly as tricky as handling a Restaurant Romeo."

"A what?" Miguel gave up all pretense of working and stared at the two women; they looked at him, then at one another and burst out laughing.

"The standard tours stick to the easier trails, but some people like more of a challenge," Dusty continued as if he hadn't spoken. Her brown eyes gleamed with suppressed laughter and he had the disconcerting feeling that the laughter was directed at him. "Like the trail over Elephant Hill, which climbs a steep, slickrock slope, then angles still higher over broken rubble. The top is a fairly flat mesa and everybody sighs with relief, but then . . ." She paused dramatically.

Miguel wanted to ask what she meant by a Restaurant Romeo, but was too caught up in her story to interrupt.

"Then," she went on, "you have to go down." She sipped at her wine, letting the suspense build. "The only way down is over a series of steep ledges and narrow switchbacks. And you have to back down one stretch."

"Definitely dangerous," Miguel decided aloud, flashing her an admiring grin.

"Exciting," Ramona chimed in.

"And you usually work at ski resorts in the winter," Miguel added before his sister could reclaim Dusty's attention. "What brings you here?"

"A friend told me about Pinecreek and it sounded like a nice change of pace." Rather than look at him, she drained her wineglass and gathered up the knapsack she carried instead of a purse. "I've got to go. Thanks for the drink."

Miguel stared after her, then turned to Ramona. "Do you realize she's worked here three days and we hardly know anything about her besides what's on her job application?" He tugged off his tie, pulled out a beer and came around the bar to sit next to his sister.

"She's a good waitress and impervious to your charm. That makes her okay in my book." She grinned saucily, but Miguel silently refused to rise to his sister's bait.

"All right," she added, relenting. "If you're going to mope, I'll find out more about her. She's certainly an improvement over the Milquetoasts you usually date."

"Both you and Dusty could take some lessons in charm from those women."

Ramona wrinkled her nose. "You mean spend our time polishing our fingernails and painting our faces? Learn how to bat our eyelashes and coo, 'Oh, Miguel, what a big, strong man you are?'"

"You exaggerate, Mona. It's you and Dusty who are extreme. You two look a man straight in the eye and feel insulted if he notices you're female."

"We want to be treated as equals."

"Equals, yes, but what's wrong with acknowledging the difference between men and women? It is, after all, what makes the world go around. By ignoring that, you're missing one of the joys in life."

"You just want to get Dusty in your bed."

Miguel grinned, but shook his head. "I'm talking about more than sex. When I open a door for a woman I'm giving her a compliment. I'm not trying to seduce her or infer that she's incapable of opening the door. Instead of glaring why can't you and Dusty say thank-you?"

Ramona rolled her eyes and sipped her wine.

"Look at Mamá." Miguel pressed on, too involved in the argument to drink his beer. "Forty-eight years old and widowed for the past twenty. She's run this restaurant and raised four children alone, but she hasn't forgotten that she's a woman. Men still jump to open doors for the pleasure of her smile."

"But she hasn't married again."

"Not for lack of opportunity. You're too young to remember Papá. They were very much in love, and it's hard for a man to compete with a ghost."

"And she's always put us and the restaurant first in her life." Ramona stared into her glass. "I wish I could remember him and how happy they were. Maybe it would make her nagging me to get married easier to take."

Miguel grinned. "A woman is not complete without a man and . . ."

"A man is not complete without a woman," Ramona finished their mother's favorite saying. She toasted him with her wineglass. "To her holdouts, you and me." She drank and set down her glass. "I'd really rather live like Dusty."

"Like a Gypsy with no place to call home? Have you noticed she's never mentioned a family? I think it would be a lonely life for you, Mona."

"I'd still like to try it. Besides, I'd have a family to come home to." She shrugged and changed the subject. "I'm surprised you're even interested in Dusty."

"I simply want to share my appreciation for the difference between the sexes with her," Miguel said, bowing his head and splaying his fingers across his chest in feigned modesty.

"She's a challenge, that's what it is," Ramona said. "Didn't you hear her call you a Restaurant Romeo? She's not going to fall for your lines."

"You think she meant me?" When his sister nodded vehemently, Miguel scowled. "That makes me sound like some kind of a promiscuous playboy."

"If the shoe fits?"

"It doesn't." He glared at her and Ramona cocked a skeptical eyebrow. "I like women," he admitted, dropping his gaze to his beer bottle, where his fingers tore at the label, "and they like me. I enjoy their company and their conversation out of bed as well as in it. From what they tell me, a lot of men don't listen to women, don't take their feelings and opinions seriously. I do."

He sipped his beer, then smiled with a mixture of pride and embarrassment. "I've found myself in the uncomfortable position of refusing a woman, believe it or not."

"I can believe it." Ramona chuckled. "I've seen you duck out the back door to avoid a woman who's been panting over the bar at you all night."

"The older I get, the choosier I get."

"You never stay with one woman long, though."

Miguel shifted uneasily on his stool and looked away. "I want to get married," he said in a quiet voice, "and watch my woman grow big with my child, have her waiting up for me when I get home at night." He sighed and took a long draw on his beer. "But when a relationship settles into a routine and I think about waking up to the same woman every morning for the rest of my life, I run like the devil."

He smiled wickedly. "Maybe I need a harem instead of a wife. I got spoiled having three sisters to look after while I was growing up."

"You mean to boss around," Ramona corrected him. "And if you're looking for a wife who will bring you your slippers," she added bluntly, "I don't think Dusty fits the bill."

"Never underestimate the power of a man over a woman."

"Or vice versa," she shot back. "I think it's more likely that *you*'ll wind up fetching *her* slippers!"

"You know me better than that."

"You could wind up getting hurt," Ramona persisted. No longer teasing, her voice was full of concern. "I don't think you'll find a relationship with Dusty boring."

"Don't worry about me, little sister. I'm a big boy. And as for Dusty not being boring . . ." He paused and clinked his glass against his sister's. "I'll drink to that."

2

DUSTY BRAKED TO A STOP and stared down the overgrown lane leading into a small canyon. She could see washboard ridges rounding the first switchback, evidence of the brief but heavy monsoon rains of summer. This descent would test both her brakes and her driving ability.

The engine of her pale yellow jeep rumbled reassuringly as she glanced at the cluster of gauges mounted low on her dashboard. All seemed well. The steep, slow climb hadn't made the engine overheat. Her father had converted the 1948 Willys Jeepster into a four-wheel drive and installed an American Motors engine. Purists of the antique car trade objected, but she loved it. The jeep took her anywhere a more expensive, brand-new vehicle would.

She didn't have time to hike down, then back up the canyon. Saturday night at La Margarita would be busy and she didn't want to be late, but she didn't want to turn around, either. In a week of searching the old mountain roads, she'd had no more luck at finding the infuriating man she sought than she'd had in putting a stop to Miguel's unwanted attentions.

Miguel attracted her, she had to admit, but she wasn't going to fall for a Restaurant Romeo with bedroom eyes and a smooth tongue. She was in Pinecreek for one reason only; that was to find the man who was some-where in these mountains, hunting for gold. And this canyon looked promising.

A trickle of a waterfall slid down the other side. Wa-ter, she'd learned, carried the gold down from the hills and deposited it in drifts and washes, if the slope wasn't too steep. This canyon flattened into a grassy meadow at the bottom, a perfect place for gold to collect.

Depressing the clutch and sliding the vehicle into first gear, she started down the hill. Hand-lettered signs ap-peared as she inched past the numerous switchbacks.

Git Back, You Ain't Wanted.

Go Away.

I Ain't Buying.

Turn Back.

The last made her smile. She couldn't turn around if she wanted to. The road was barely wide enough for her jeep, and at every bend she prayed she wouldn't find a boulder or downed tree in her path. Backing up the rutted curves was not a pleasant prospect.

As she descended, the reddish bark of ponderosa pines and the white trunks of aspen gave way to piñon pines and junipers mixed with Gambel oaks, prickly pear cactus and manzanita. Cottonwoods and syca-mores lined the stream on the canyon floor, while the purple of wild asters and the yellow of goldeneye spiked the tall grass of the green meadow.

A rickety, wooden bridge spanned the shallow, sluggish stream. A sign hanging on a chain across it warned her not to trespass. Like the other signs, the paint was old and faded. Whoever had made them was long gone, Dusty thought. This was a perfect site for the squatter she hoped to find.

Tire tracks leading to the right of the bridge assured her that she wouldn't be the first to ignore the signs, so she followed them across the stream and through the meadow to the opposite side of the canyon. Tucked among the tall trees was a tiny log cabin with a tin roof. Smoke rose from its chimney, but she saw no trace of the old, familiar pickup. Probably hidden behind the shack, she figured, her heart beating with anticipation.

Stopping the Willys, she climbed out and approached the cabin. He'd made himself right at home, she reflected, glancing around. A hand-operated pump indicated the presence of a well and fresh drinking water. A claw-foot bathtub sat nearby, buckets lined up neatly beside it. A garden grew behind a fence made of sticks. Logs cut to serve as stools surrounded a fire pit complete with a grill and a spit for roasting meat. Chickens pecked the ground next to the firewood stacked alongside the house. A rocking chair sat on the small porch.

But where was Cody? she wondered as she set foot on the first step. The door was open, and surely the dog could hear or scent her by now.

She peered inside the cabin, waiting to speak until her eyes grew accustomed to the shaded interior. Light from one small window silhouetted a figure bent over a wood stove, its back to her. Too short, she realized. Disappointment seared her and she stepped back, bumping into the rocking chair.

The man spun around, a spatula in his hand. "Who in the blue blazes are you? Cain't you read? This here is private property!"

Brandishing the spatula, he advanced on her and Dusty backed down the steps. "I'm sorry," she said hastily, "but I'm looking for someone. I know he's in this area somewhere, but I'm not sure where." She reached into the breast pocket of her shirt and pulled out a photograph. "Please, have you seen him?"

The old man ignored the picture and glared at her. His eyes were a faded blue beneath bushy, black eyebrows, although his cheeks bristled with white whiskers that matched his unkempt hair. His gray undershirt was frayed and patched, but clean, as were the shapeless black pants hanging from his skinny hips.

"He's my father," Dusty added softly, "Jack Rose."

The old man slowly lowered the spatula. "Come on in whilst I take the beans and bacon off the fire. Don't want to burn my supper." She followed him into the one-room cabin. A cot stood along one wall, neatly topped with an old army blanket. A worn, plastic tablecloth covered a picnic table near the stove. A counter with a dry sink lay beneath cabinets of rough pine. The man slammed pots and pans around on the cast-iron stove and grumbled under his breath about his cabin being like Grand Central Station.

"My eyes ain't what they used to be," he muttered, turning and leading her back to the sunlight on the porch. He took the photograph she held and squinted at it. His fingers were thick and gnarled with old age and hard work.

"Yep. I seen him." He handed back the picture, dug into his pocket and pulled out a tin of chewing tobacco. Dusty shook her head when he offered it to her.

"When? Where?" Questions crowded into her mind as she tucked the picture back into her pocket, but the old man refused to be rushed. He stuck a pinch of tobacco into his mouth and settled himself in the rocking chair.

"Durned dog chased my chickens and they didn't lay for a week." He rocked to the rhythm of his chewing.

"That sounds like Cody," Dusty murmured, as she sat down at the top of the steps and stared at the sunlit meadow. She felt light-headed with relief. Her father was alive!

"Yep, that was his name. Looked like a mangy old coyote, 'cept for the beard on his muzzle and his ears kind of sat up on his head, 'specially when Happy Jack pulled out his guitar."

"You do know them!" Dusty turned to smile at him.

"Did ya think I was lying, girl?" He spat a stream of tobacco juice into an old coffee can on the porch and leaned forward in his chair to face her indignantly.

"No, no," she assured him. "I believed you, but Jack and Cody don't sing for just anybody. They must have really liked you. And only Dad's best friends call him Happy Jack."

"Sure, they liked me." Mollified, he resumed his rocking. "That Cody'd stick his nose up to the moon and just yip and howl right along with the music." He shook his head. "They ain't been by for a spell. Been kinda expecting them."

Dusty felt her smile grow dim. "How long has it been?"

The old man scratched his head. "Don't rightly know for sure. Was sick a while back and lost track of time. I'd say two, three weeks." He lowered his hand to the arm of the chair, his face scrunched up in thought, then he shrugged.

"Nuthin' to worry about, girl. Happy Jack can take care of hisself. A good man, he is. Done built me a coop for my chickens so's Cody couldn't bother them none when they come visitin'. Didn't trust him right off when he first came, though."

"When was that?"

He thought for a moment. "Back when the weather first warmed. Wanted to know all 'bout prospecting. Knew enuff to see I got a good place but not a durned thing 'bout panning or dry-washing. Thought he wanted to rob me at first, then he offered to pay for his lessons with work and whiskey." He spat another stream of tobacco juice into the can. "Durned good whiskey, too." His pale eyes gleamed. "Not like—"

"Do you know where he is?" Dusty interrupted with an anxious glance at the lowering sun. She didn't have time to listen to whiskey tales. She had to get to work.

"He never rightly said, but I told him to try over on the east side of the mountains by Bear Creek."

"Could you show me on a map?" Dusty stood. "I've got one in my car."

"Sure enough."

He shuffled into the cabin, then met her at the jeep with a magnifying glass. They spread the map out on the hood and he pinpointed the area. Although not small, it narrowed the range of her search considerably and Dusty thanked him heartily.

"I don't even know your name," she said, folding up the map and tossing it onto the front seat. Leaving the car door open, she extended her hand, then winced at the surprising strength of his grip.

"Henry," he said, "but Jack called me Hank. And you're Dusty, right?" He barely waited for her nod. "Your father was real proud of you. Said you was better than any son could be. You bring him back with you when you find him and I'll roast us a chicken with all the trimmin's."

Pleased to hear of her father's praise, Dusty hugged him. A girl's place was with her mother, Jack had said when she was ten and her parents had divorced. By implication she'd known if she'd been a boy, he would have fought for more than summer custody. And she wouldn't have had to spend those miserable school years in Newark, New Jersey.

Hank patted her back awkwardly. "Everything will be fine," he said, reading her hug as a need for comfort. "Don't you worry none. Just tell Jack to bring his guitar and Cody and we'll have a howling good time." He chuckled at his own joke.

Dusty smiled and climbed behind the steering wheel. "We'll bring some of that good whiskey, too."

"Now, you're talking, girl! Jack done raised you right. Now git going, so's you can hurry back."

With a smile and a wave, she put the jeep into gear and headed back up the canyon.

THE CLOCK READ ten minutes before five when Dusty rushed into La Margarita's kitchen. "You're late," he told her as he entered from the dining room and set down his plate. His gaze swept her from head to toe, then lingered on the legs bared by her cutoffs.

"I've got ten minutes to change," Dusty said, holding up her work clothes and hurrying past him.

"Personally, I prefer you the way you are."

"They're only legs," she snapped over her shoulder.

"They're lovely."

Dusty swung around to glare at him. "Thank you. They come in handy for walking." Miguel smiled pleased at getting a rise out of her. "You're impossible," she muttered and pushed through the swinging doors into the dining room.

At the sight of her, Mamá Rosa rose from the table nearest the kitchen where the employees were eating their dinner together. This did not look like the affable, motherly woman Dusty had come to know. This was a boss, an angry boss.

"You are late," she announced and lapsed into a torrent of Spanish. She stomped around the table and came to a stop in front of Dusty. At five feet tall, the older woman had to look up at her, nonetheless Mamá Rosa waved an admonishing finger under Dusty's nose. Dusty heard the kitchen door swing open behind her, then felt Miguel's breath brush her cheek even before he spoke.

"She says you are irresponsible," he explained. "She's been worried sick that Luisa would have to wait tables instead of hostessing, and you would cause her to lose her first baby. She is sure you have turned her hair gray."

The woman before her gestured toward a crown of shining hair as dark as her children's, then settled her hands upon her hips. Mamá Rosa looked younger than her years and took pride in her appearance. Her ample curves could easily have run to fat, but she'd kept herself trim. Dusty, on the other hand, she constantly told to eat more.

Mamá Rosa was doing just that now. Miguel relayed his mother's dismay that she'd missed her dinner. She opened her mouth to lie and say she'd already eaten, but he stopped her.

"Don't speak until she's done. You'll make her angrier."

Not knowing what else to do, Dusty obeyed, uncomfortably aware of Miguel's closeness. He rested one hand on her shoulder while he spoke into her ear. The warmth of his palm spread a flush across her flesh. He rolled his r's in a musical cadence, and the meaning of the words he uttered blurred in her mind into the caressing tones of a lover.

Mamá Rosa paused in her tirade. Did she expect an answer? Startled, Dusty glanced at Miguel, hoping she hadn't missed the question. He smiled at her reassuringly and answered his mother without looking away from Dusty.

"*Sí, Mamá, tengo mucho interés en esta Dusty Rose.*"

Dusty heard Ramona laugh and turned toward her. Her friend winked, but did not translate. No one did. All Dusty had understood was her name.

"Then I will not fire you," Mamá Rosa said, her face suddenly wreathed in smiles as she slipped back into English. "But you will explain why you are late, then we will be sure this does not happen again."

Unwilling to share the story of her father, Dusty had rehearsed her lies on the drive to work, but found they did not slip easily from her tongue when she faced Mamá Rosa's penetrating dark eyes. "I had a flat tire," she said, forcing her gaze not to waver. "I changed it as fast as I could and hurried here rather than look for a telephone."

"Call next time."

Dusty let her gaze drop. "Yes, ma'am, I'm sorry."

Mamá Rosa patted her cheek. "It is forgotten, these things happen." She turned to the group still at the table. "The show is over, get those things cleared away. Carlos, reset the table. Luisa, unlock the front door. Carmen, get into the kitchen and be ready for orders. I will join you shortly. Ramona, you take the early tables while Dusty eats."

"I'll just change clothes," Dusty protested.

"You will eat first." Mamá Rosa took her by the arm and led her into the kitchen. "It is not healthy to work on an empty stomach, and how will you keep a man's interest if you stay so skinny?"

Dusty ate quickly, but Mamá Rosa still wasn't finished with her. "It is Saturday night, fiesta time, and you must look especially nice. Come over to the house with me. You will change your clothes and I will fix you up."

When they recrossed the small courtyard that separated Mamá Rosa's house from the restaurant, Dusty wore pink ribbons woven into her braid, brown eye shadow and mascara, blush on her cheeks, pink lipstick and gold hoop earrings. She'd heard all she ever wanted to hear about pleasing a man. She would, she decided, kiss her father when she found him, then strangle him with her bare hands. The wolf whistles the teenage dishwashers delivered as she passed through the kitchen did not improve her mood.

"I feel like a trussed-up chicken," she hissed at Ramona when she joined her at the waitress station in the dining room. "Don't you dare laugh."

"May I smile broadly?" Ramona asked, doing exactly that as she handed her a stack of napkins.

"Why doesn't she paint your face?" Dusty asked, automatically folding the napkins into the accordion pleats that made them stand, fan shaped, upright on the tables.

"I'm not her prospective daughter-in-law."

"What!"

"Lower your voice, the whole dining room can hear you." Ramona kept her eyes on the napkins she was folding, but Dusty saw a smile lift the corners of her lips. She stepped closer to the younger girl. Ramona was the tallest of the Santiago women, but Dusty towered over her by at least six inches.

"If you don't tell me, right now, what you meant by that crack," she threatened through gritted teeth, "I'm going to step on you and squash you like a bug."

"Ladies never resort to physical violence," Ramona said primly, her dark eyes flashing with laughter.

"Whoever said I was a lady?"

"You look like one at the moment."

Dusty groaned. "Would she fire me if I washed my face?"

"Not if Miguel asked her not to."

"What does Miguel have to do with this?"

"Mamá stopped in the middle of her tantrum and asked him if he was interested in you." Ramona eyed her slyly. "You did look very nice standing together, your blond head so close to his dark one. And you were all dreamy-eyed...."

"I was not! He was translating for me."

"Sure looked like he was whispering sweet nothings in your ear and you liked it."

"He wasn't and I didn't!"

Ramona smiled again and Dusty caught herself. She was overreacting and Ramona knew it. She *had* been affected by Miguel's closeness, but wasn't about to admit it. "So what did Miguel say?"

"Yes, obviously. Why do you think you're still here and all gussied up?"

Glaring at Ramona, Dusty grabbed a napkin, balled it in her fist and threw it onto the floor. "I am not putting this junk on my face every night, and these earrings are pulling my ears down to my knees!"

"Miguel isn't really so bad, I've known him all my life. Give him half a chance."

"Read my lips," Dusty snapped, then enunciated her next words slowly and clearly. "I...am... not...interested." Swiveling rapidly, she stomped to the bar.

As usual, Miguel grinned at her, then performed an exaggerated double take of surprise at her appearance. "I didn't think it possible to improve on such beauty."

For the benefit of the two customers at the other end of the bar, Dusty stretched her lips into a parody of a smile. "Miguel, could you come a little closer, please?"

"Your wish is my command." He stepped in front of her. "It is a pleasure to hear my name on your lips. You know, I think this is the first time you've used it in the five days you've worked here."

"Closer, please," she said, leaning over the bar. He moved with her, stopping only when their faces were inches apart. "I want you," she began in a sultry voice, then paused and switched to a fierce whisper, "to go to hell!"

"Such passion," he murmured. Before she could withdraw, his hands whipped out to cup her face, and he dropped a quick kiss upon her lips. The men at the other end of the bar applauded.

Dusty stepped back as soon as he released her. "I could sue you for sexual harassment," she hissed, rubbing the back of her hand over her mouth.

"And I could fire you for insubordination, but this is getting much too interesting to end it now, don't you think?" His dark eyes danced. "Lighten up, Dusty. I'm only flirting with you. What are you afraid of?"

She lifted her chin. "Not you, that's for sure."

"Then you're afraid of yourself. Scared you might like me if you got to know me?"

"Not a chance."

His grin widened. Her insults slid off him like oil on a wet surface. Shaking her head, she turned to go.

"Oh, Dusty," he called and she reluctantly looked back. He wiped his lips with a paper napkin and extended it to her. "Your lipstick is smeared."

Glaring at him, she snatched a napkin from the pile and strode away. Savagely rubbing her lips, she wished she could also erase the memory of his lips on hers.

By seven o'clock the restaurant and bar were full and people were waiting for tables. Dusty didn't have time to think, but Mamá Rosa managed to remind her three times to put on more lipstick. Whenever she went to the bar to get drinks, Miguel eyed her lips and grinned again.

By the time her last table emptied, Dusty longed to take every bottle in the bar and break them over his head. Maybe not every bottle, she silently amended, when Mamá Rosa herded her toward the bar for a cozy nightcap with her son; she'd save several for his mother.

"It is a tradition for us to gather on Saturday night," the older woman insisted, but Dusty saw Luisa and Carmen putting on their jackets and bidding their brother good-night. Ramona had already deserted her in favor of meeting some friends, and Mamá Rosa, Dusty figured, would disappear the second she sat down.

"It's been a very long day," Dusty said firmly, "and I'm tired. One drink and I wouldn't be safe driving home." She ducked under the bar and retrieved her knapsack. She saw Miguel's long, black-clad legs approaching and retreated hastily. "See you Tuesday night," she said, smiling at the sight of Mamá Rosa's frustrated expression.

She was shivering when she reached the parking lot. She hadn't thought to grab a jacket when she left her apartment that morning. September days in the Arizona mountains were still warm, but the temperature dropped fast when the sun went down. Eagerly she unlocked the Willys and climbed behind the steering wheel. Jamming the key into the ignition, she turned it and pressed the accelerator.

The engine turned, whirred . . . and died. "C'mon, baby," Dusty muttered, turning the key again. "I'm cold, too. Let's get warm together." The engine whirred, sputtered . . . and died. "Dammit!" she exploded and slammed her fist against the steering wheel. "You can't fail me now!" Only one other car remained in the parking lot—an electric-blue Mazda Miata with a black convertible top. She didn't have to be Sherlock Holmes to figure out who owned it. She wasn't about to let Restaurant Romeo rush to her rescue.

Inhaling a huge breath, she calmed herself. Maybe a week of driving dirt roads had clogged the air filter. Pulling her tool kit and flashlight from the back seat, she braced herself against the cold, then climbed out of the jeep and opened the hood. With the help of the wan illumination of the streetlight and her flashlight, she found the proper screws and pulled out the filter. While it wasn't exactly clean, she could at least see light through it.

Frowning and shivering, she checked the spark plugs, breaker points and condenser, then searched the vacuum lines for splits or breaks. Nothing. Neither could she see any fuel leaks around the engine or on the ground.

Fighting the growing suspicion that the problem was something she couldn't fix, she tightened every screw and bolt she could find in the hope that the rough roads had loosened a connection. Closing the hood, she climbed back into the Willys.

Rubbing her bare arms for warmth, she offered a silent prayer, then turned the key in the ignition again. No change. It had to be the fuel system. A clogged line or filter, if she was lucky. Worse, a defective pump. Worse yet, a bad carburetor.

She didn't feel lucky, not the way her day had gone since leaving Hank's canyon. In any case, there was nothing more she could do. That meant a tow truck. A garage. Repair bills. And tomorrow was Sunday, so the soonest it could be worked on was Monday.

Her two days off. Two days she'd planned to spend searching for her father. Instead, she'd have to spend them staring at the four walls of her one-room apartment.

How could her Willys fail her on this night of all nights? After the emotional ups and downs of the long day, she couldn't fight her bitter disappointment. Laying her head upon the steering wheel, she cried, hating the hot tears that slid down her cheeks.

Suddenly she heard a light rapping on her closed window. Vaguely she heard her name being called. She pulled a tissue from her knapsack, blew her nose and raised her head.

"Dusty, are you all right?" Miguel's concerned face stared at her through the window.

3

DUSTY JERKED BACK, first in surprise, then in anger. She'd forgotten all about the other car in the parking lot. "I'm fine!" she yelled, hastily dropping the tissue. "Go away!" Averting her face, she swiped at her wet cheeks with her hands.

Miguel opened the car door. "Are you deaf?" she snapped.

"Has anyone ever told you you're very bad-tempered?" he asked, propping an elbow on the top of the car door and a foot on the running board.

"I've had a bad day, I'm tired, and I don't feel like fencing with you."

"Fencing?" His familiar grin appeared; apparently he approved of her choice of words. "You are on guard, aren't you?"

Too tired to think of a snappy comeback, Dusty stared at him. His leather bomber jacket made his shoulders appear even broader and his hips narrower. His shirt collar was open, with no gold chain in sight. The streetlight illuminated his handsome features, but the darkness inside the car hid her reddened eyes and nose. She hoped.

"Are you having car trouble?" he asked.

No, I like to sit and freeze in parking lots, Dusty wanted to answer. "Yes," she said, realizing that as much as she hated to ask anything of him, she had to get to a telephone. "Can you let me back in the restaurant so I can call a tow truck?"

"At midnight? Why don't I take a look?"

"Gas isn't getting to the engine. I'm sure it's the fuel system. I've checked the air filter and just about everything else." She shivered, suddenly aware again of the cold.

"It takes two to check that. Start her up." Miguel stepped back and opened the hood.

Dusty decided it was easier to obey than argue. Listening to the engine sputter and die, she didn't notice Miguel shrug out of his jacket.

"Sure you've got gas?" He reached inside the car and laid the jacket around her shoulders.

"Of course." She bit back her irritation. He was trying to help, she reminded herself, and the fleece lining of his jacket, still warm from his body heat, felt wonderful against her chilled flesh. "Now you'll be cold," she protested halfheartedly.

"I have on long sleeves." He moved back to the open hood. "I don't smell gas. You haven't flooded it."

"I know." Dusty slipped her arms into the jacket and zipped it up. If he wanted to play macho and freeze when she'd already told him what the problem with the car was, that was his problem. In the meantime, she might as well be comfortable.

The leather was soft from use, enfolding her smaller frame. It smelled faintly of after-shave, which she'd always dismissed as perfume for men, but she had to admit she liked this light, masculine scent.

"I think it's the carburetor," he concluded, slamming the hood down with a bang. "Do you have a rag for my hands?"

Dusty sighed glumly and handed him several tissues. As she'd feared, the problem was one she couldn't fix herself. "I'll call a tow truck. Thanks for your help." She pulled the keys from the ignition, gathered up her knapsack and climbed out, locking the door behind her. She headed for the restaurant, but he caught her arm and steered her toward his sports car.

"I'll drive you home," he said. "I doubt there's a twenty-four-hour towing service and even if there is, they'd charge you an arm and a leg for it. No one will work on it until Monday, anyway."

He opened the passenger door of his car. Although still warmed by his jacket, she shivered. The prospect of spending time alone with him unsettled her. Dusty shook her head. "I want it worked on first thing Monday morning. I'd rather have it there as soon as possible."

"We can get it to a garage tomorrow." He stepped back from the door and nudged her toward the car seat, one hand on the small of her back.

We? Dusty silently echoed, allowing him to ease her into the car. She didn't have the energy to argue. If he wouldn't let her back into the restaurant to get to a telephone, she'd have to pound on Mamá Rosa's door, and she'd want to know why Dusty didn't let Miguel drive her home.

Compared to her heavy, high-set jeep, the sports car felt like a tin can and the seats were also far too close together. Miguel's shoulder brushed against hers as he slid behind the steering wheel and she shrank closer to her door, then reared back still farther when he reached for her.

"Hold still," he said, "blackface doesn't become you." He gently wiped her cheeks with a tissue.

"I must have brushed my hair back without cleaning my hands," Dusty said, although she figured she'd dirtied her face when she'd tried to hide her tears.

"You weren't crying?"

"Not over a broken-down car." And she hadn't been, Dusty assured herself; she'd been crying about losing two full days in the search for her father.

He cocked a skeptical eyebrow, turned away and dropped his hand to the gearshift. Dusty eased her legs away from him.

"Still on guard?"

"I didn't want to get in your way." Because she felt awkward, she added, "I'm not used to such a small car. I feel like I'm sitting on the ground." Then she bit her lip. She hadn't meant to belittle his car.

"Think you've come down in the world?" Miguel asked, a smile in his voice.

"In perspective, yes," she assured him, glad he hadn't taken offense. "In luxury I've come up." The bucket seats were contoured and covered in real leather, she noticed, and the powerful engine purred when he pulled out of the parking lot. "It certainly rides more smoothly than Willys." He turned toward the downtown section, and she supposed he'd ask for directions when they reached Main Street.

"A little newer, I imagine."

"Willy's newer than he looks. About the only thing original on him is the body and that's been refinished. This is the first time he's failed me in four years."

"Who restored it?"

"My father. I thought he'd been working on it for himself, but he surprised me by making it a present for my twenty-first birthday." The reminder silenced her until Miguel turned left rather than right on Main Street.

"I live the other way," she said.

"I ordered a pizza. It'll only take a minute to pick up."

Dusty waited in the car while Miguel went inside the pizza parlor. He'd left the engine running and heat poured out of the vents. She should, she told herself, take his jacket off, the better to make a quick escape when they reached her home, but couldn't bring herself to do it. She liked the feel of it. Not only was it warm, it made her feel small, practically petite, and well—her mind stumbled over other, unfamiliar feelings—feminine, coddled, protected.

Weak.

Her hand flew to the zipper at her throat. The car door opened and Miguel plopped a boxed pizza into her lap and a bag onto the floor at her feet. "Where do we go from here?" he asked. Dusty gave him directions.

"Thanks for the ride," she said, as he pulled up in front of the old Victorian house divided into apartments. He ignored the pizza box she pushed toward him and got out.

She handed him the box when he opened her door. "I'm sure you want to get home before the pizza gets cold," she said, unzipping the jacket and shrugging out of it as she left the car. "I won't keep you." She tried to give him the jacket, but he was holding the pizza with both hands.

"Why don't you invite me in and share it with me?" he suggested. "I bought some beer, too." Holding the pizza with one hand now, he ducked past her and reached into the car, pulling out her knapsack and the bag he'd set upon the floor. Handing her the knapsack, he closed and locked the door, then grinned expectantly at her.

"I'm really not hungry," Dusty said.

"Then you can keep me company," he said, turning in the direction of the house. "It's depressing to eat alone." Dusty glared at his back, then sighed and followed him.

MIGUEL STARED in astonishment at the bare room. A sleeping bag and a pillow lay atop a foam rubber pad on the carpeted floor. A wind-up clock, a propane lantern and two small, framed pictures sat on an ice chest beside it. A guitar stood propped against one wall and a breakfast bar separated the room from a tiny kitchenette, but no stools to provide seating.

"Silverware is in the drawer to the left of the sink," Dusty said. "Napkins are on the counter and plates are in the cabinet by the refrigerator. If you sit on the bed, the cooler serves as a table." She crossed the room and closed the drapes over a big bay window, the only thing that saved the room from looking like a cell.

"Make yourself at home," she said, opening a door in the back of an alcove. "I can't stand these clothes."

"Slipping into something more comfortable?" Miguel asked. Her answer was the click of the lock on what he realized was the bathroom door. She didn't trust him an inch. Chuckling and shaking his head, he crossed to the kitchen and set the beer and pizza upon the counter.

Her silverware, he discovered, was of the flat, lightweight, camping variety, as were her few dishes. He washed the stain of car grease from his hands in the sink, then popped open two beers and put the rest in a refrigerator, as bare as the room. A carton of milk and a bottle of apple juice shared a shelf with jars of mustard, mayonnaise and a package of lunch meat.

Still hoping she'd eat with him, he slid the pizza into the oven, which he set on Warm, and carried the beers to the cooler. He lighted the lantern, then turned off the overhead light and sat down on the makeshift bed. Offering a silent toast, he congratulated himself on his entry into Dusty's den and took a long swallow of his beer. His grin faded when his gaze fell upon the photographs perched on the ice chest.

One was of a radiant Dusty in a man's embrace. Setting down his beer, he picked up the picture and studied it in the soft glow of the lantern. Her father, he decided, relaxing. His beard and longish hair were the same deep blond hue as Dusty's and his eyes the same warm chocolate. Even their tans matched. And she'd clearly inherited her height from him. Cliffs and a river in the background made him suspect the photograph was taken in Utah. Maybe she did have family there and wasn't quite the homeless Gypsy he'd thought.

Cocking an ear toward the bathroom, he reached for the other photograph. The drumming of the shower told him that Dusty wouldn't be joining him anytime soon. He would, he mused, prefer to join her. A credit card would easily open a bathroom lock. Did he dare?

No. Judging by her jumpiness around him, she wasn't as immune to him as she wanted him to think...but she was not a woman to be rushed. He'd have to move slowly, get to know her better. He grinned, remembering his conversation with Ramona.

Because he genuinely liked women and cared about what they had to say, seduction had become ridiculously easy, even unintended at times. But he'd never lied, had never made false promises. Once or twice he'd thought he'd found love, but had made no rash declarations. In time, routine and boredom had crept into each relationship.

He couldn't imagine that seducing Dusty Rose would be easy or that he'd ever find her boring. He wasn't about to risk losing the chance to find out by rushing her. Rather than dwelling on the tantalizing image of her in the shower, he forced himself to focus on the second picture.

This one was of a family standing on a green lawn in front of a two-story brick house. Dusty wasn't part of the picture. A paunchy man with thinning hair stood with his arm around a petite, elegant blonde. Three small children were lined up in front of them. None bore any resemblance to Dusty.

The shower stopped and he replaced the photograph on the cooler. Propping the pillow against the wall, he leaned back and waited patiently. He knew she probably hoped he'd eat and leave. But she was in for a surprise. He had no intention of leaving before breakfast.

DUSTY FELT immeasurably better when she stepped out of the shower, her face scrubbed clean of makeup, car grease and tear stains. Slipping into her black sweat suit, she smiled to herself, imagining Miguel's disappointment. He probably hoped she'd come out in a black negligee.

"A vision of loveliness," he pronounced, rising from the bed and bringing her a beer as she opened the bathroom door. "And in record time, too."

"Eat your pizza," she retorted, confident that her sweat suit was as sexy as a sack.

"Join me," he said, escorting her to the makeshift table. "Do you like *jalapeño* and pineapple?"

"I've never had it," she said, sitting cross-legged on the far side of the cooler, careful to avoid the bed. "Sounds weird." The gentle glow of the propane lantern made the setting too intimate for her taste. She turned up the flame.

"The hot and sweet blend nicely on the tongue. Try some." He crossed to the kitchen and brought back napkins and the pizza while she cleared off the top of the ice chest.

"You play the guitar?" He indicated the instrument with a wave of the pizza slice he passed to her.

"A little. It comes in handy on overnight tours. It's amazing how people are at a loss for entertainment without television." She took a small bite of the pizza. Miguel's gaze followed the path of the cheese stretching from the pizza to her lips. She raised her hand and quickly popped the rest into her mouth.

"It's good," she admitted, reaching for her beer. Miguel nodded and smiled. "Hot," she said, "but good."

"Who's the family?" Miguel asked after a few minutes, indicating the photographs she'd set aside.

"The Oh-So Rights," she answered, chuckling at her private joke. Miguel cocked an eyebrow questioningly. "That's what my dad calls them. It's my mother's second marriage. Her husband's name is Fred Wright, with a W. He's an insurance salesman in New Jersey." She wrinkled her nose in a gesture of distaste.

"Your stepfather."

Dusty shook her head vehemently. "My mother's husband." She reached for another slice of pizza, then hesitated. "Do you mind?"

"There's plenty, help yourself." He picked up the other photograph. "But you're very close to your real father?"

"Yes." She summoned a smile. She didn't want to think about her father.

"And where does he live?"

"Wherever the spirit moves him." She blinked rapidly and took another bite of pizza, although she hadn't swallowed the last one. Why couldn't the guy shut up and eat?

"Quite the opposite of an insurance salesman in New Jersey," Miguel observed.

Dusty laughed. "You got that right. Fred's idea of experiencing nature is a trip to a crowded beach."

"And your father's?"

"Backpacking as 'far from the madding crowd' as he can get."

"In New Jersey?" he asked.

Dusty shook her head. "In Dad's opinion, the country ceases to exist east of the Mississippi River."

"Where did you live? With your mother or your father?"

Dusty sipped her beer, then leaned back. "What is this, 'Twenty Questions?'"

Miguel shrugged. "I've lived in Pinecreek all my life except for the four years I went to college in Tucson. You fascinate me."

Dusty was unconvinced. "You want my life story at—" she glanced at the bedside clock "—one o'clock in the morning?" She gathered up their napkins and closed the pizza box in a signal of dismissal.

"I'm a night owl. I need a bedtime story before I sleep."

"Don't even think about falling asleep in my bed."

"Join me?"

"Not a chance."

He grinned and Dusty found herself smiling. His good humor was infectious and she had to admit, he wasn't hitting on her very hard. She'd thought he'd start groping for her as soon as they got in the door.

"So, once upon a time . . ." Miguel prompted, making it obvious he wouldn't leave until she'd told her story.

Dusty sighed. "I need another beer if I'm going to play true confessions."

"Where's a good waitress when you need one?" Miguel asked, looking around in feigned disgust.

"Yeah," Dusty agreed cheerfully, "the service in this joint is lousy. I work all night and have to come home and serve myself, aching feet and all."

Miguel took the hint and went to the kitchen. Dusty claimed his place on the bed and pointed to the spot she'd vacated when he returned with their beers. Ignoring her directive, he sat down on the end of the bed.

Dusty tucked up her feet, but he pulled them back to his lap. "My payment for your life story is a foot massage." He pulled off one sock. Dusty froze. But her alarm dissolved as his thumbs kneaded her sole, finding pressure points that relaxed her whole body.

"Once upon a time, there was a little girl named Dusty Rose . . ." he began.

How was she supposed to talk beneath the magic of his massage? she wondered. All she wanted to do was close her eyes and feel his wonderful touch climb up her aching calves, knees, thighs. . . . She widened her eyes at that thought and quickly picked up his cue.

"Dusty's parents were Jack and Bonnie," she began, "who never should have met, much less married and had a baby. But away from her family for the first time, the college girl from New Jersey found Jack's park ranger uniform and the Grand Canyon a romantic combination. Jack had a weakness for blue-eyed blondes and they were married by the time Bonnie's summer job ended. What Bonnie hadn't realized was that Jack's job ended, too."

She paused while Miguel gently rotated her foot, first in one direction, then the other. Her ankle made little popping sounds as he worked out the kinks. If he could perform such wonders on her feet, what could he do with the rest of her body? She forced her mind back on track. "Dad was a seasonal park ranger, you see. He could do just about anything he set his mind to, but he didn't like to do it in one place too long. Mom thought marriage meant babies and a house with a white picket fence. I arrived a year later."

A sigh of pure pleasure escaped her; Miguel had transferred his attention to her other foot. "Dad got his way those first few years—winters in Mexico, summers in places as different as Glacier National Park in Montana and Canyonlands in Utah. But the battle lines were drawn. Mother and he would have terrible fights. Then Dad would take me hiking or camping until she cooled down." She took a deep breath.

"Are you bored yet?"

Miguel shook his head. His dark eyes were alive with interest and his smile was full of encouragement. Dusty sipped her beer. He was either sincere or a very good actor, she decided. "When I turned six, my mother dropped the bomb. Now that I was school age, it was time to settle down. Dad tried, he really did, but by the time I was ten, we'd moved four times. He just couldn't tolerate an indoor job or a boss looking over his shoulder eight hours a day. My mother left him and we went to live with her parents in Newark, New Jersey until she met and married Fred."

"And neither New Jersey nor Fred could compare to your father," Miguel guessed. He'd finished her massage, but still cradled her feet in his lap.

"My dad could name every plant, bird or animal in the West. Fred could barely recognize a marigold." Dusty sat up and crossed her legs. "And it wasn't long before my mother tried to turn me into a cheerleader!" she added indignantly. "I was tall and wanted to play basketball, but she wanted me to wear short skirts and wave pom-poms."

"A fate worse than death," Miguel agreed solemnly, then exploded into laughter.

"To me it was," Dusty insisted, but her lips curved into a smile. "So I didn't do either." She yawned, pulled her braid over her shoulder and flopped back onto the pillow. "I got to play Mother's helper after school, instead. Three babies in six years kept Mom—and me—pretty busy." She removed the rubber band from her hair and began unbraiding it. "And that's when I decided I never wanted a life like my mother's. That's it. Time for good little boys to go home, so I can get some sleep."

"Did you still get to see your father?"

"Every summer." She yawned again and glanced pointedly at the bedside clock. "I felt like a Ping-Pong ball, bouncing between yin and yang. Fun and games in the great outdoors with Dad. Housework, babies and school with Mom. When I graduated from high school, she wanted me to go to secretarial school and live at home." She frowned.

"Dad wanted me to go to college, but when I told him I couldn't bear to be confined within four walls any longer, he helped me get my first job in Moab. I crewed on raft trips down the Colorado River and never went back to Newark."

"And now?"

The hands on her braid grew still, and her gaze dropped to her lap. "I haven't seen him since last spring."

Miguel reached out to stroke her cheek. "Where is he?"

Dusty couldn't resist the gentle gesture. She turned her face into the warmth of his hand, just for a minute. Then she took a deep breath and lifted her head. "Here, somewhere, looking for gold instead of searching for Indian ruins in Utah, like he usually does."

She sighed and looked away. "He's found Anasazi cliff dwellings and Fremont pictographs never before discovered. Prehistoric Indian culture fascinates him, but he gave it up because there's no money in it. He's not a *pothunter*." She laced the term with scorn and turned her attention back to Miguel. "There's a big black market for artifacts, but he'd never desecrate the sites or steal from them."

"Jack Rose sounds like an interesting man," Miguel murmured.

"He's not exactly conventional. Searching for gold is his version of preparing for old age." She paused. "Neither is he very dependable."

Abruptly she stood up and started pacing. "But he's never let me down before!" With her defenses weakened by Miguel's attentions, she couldn't stop her anger and frustration from spilling out. "He left Moab last spring, before I got back from Snowbird ski resort. He wrote and said he was going prospecting in Pinecreek, but would be back for our birthdays. We were both born September first. I was turning twenty-five and he was turning fifty. My quarter and his half century seemed like milestones." Her pacing accelerated with her words. "He was really excited about some ruins he'd found and he promised to take me to see them when he got back.

"The man never showed! I waited a week, but he didn't call or write. I got so mad, I came down here to find him. All he has for an address is a post office box, so I've been searching the old mining roads." As suddenly as her anger had risen, it drained away. She flopped back onto the bed and pulled the pillow into her lap.

"I found an old miner today who gave me a lead—and wouldn't you know it, Willys breaks down on me!" She tossed the pillow into the air in a gesture of frustration. Miguel regarded her thoughtfully.

"What do you think?" she asked, but didn't wait for an answer. "I've been seriously considering patricide, myself. As soon as I get my hands on him, I'm going to wring his neck."

Miguel smiled slightly and leaned forward. "I think," he said softly as his hands finished unraveling her braid, "you need a friend with a four-wheel-drive truck." Dusty held herself very still. The light brushing of his fingers through her hair sparked a tingling that traveled from her scalp to her toes.

Dusty stared at his mouth, hovering inches from hers. The distance between them slowly narrowed, and she closed her eyes. His lips touched hers in a caress so light that it tickled the sensitive skin and tantalized her, leaving her longing for more. Eyes still closed, she ran her tongue across her lips, savoring the lingering sensation. When he spoke again his voice sounded far away.

"What time shall we start tomorrow?"

4

DUSTY OPENED HER EYES and stared at Miguel. His lips were curved in a sensual half smile, making it difficult for her to grasp the meaning of the words he'd uttered.

"You don't have a truck," she finally said.

"No, but Carmen's husband does. He'd be happy to trade me for a few days."

Dusty didn't want a truck; she wanted another kiss. Her senses clamored and screamed for it, and she continued to stare at his lips. A real kiss—deep, consuming and hot. "Why...?" She cleared her throat, as if that act would also clear her muddled mind. "Why would you want to do that?"

His smile broadened. "Isn't it obvious? I'd like to get to know you better."

Dusty rolled off the bed and rose to a standing position, towering over him. "You mean you'll help me look for my father," she snapped, "if I go to bed with you?"

Miguel's smile vanished. He sat back against the wall and crossed his arms over his chest. "I'd like to make love to you, yes. But I didn't have payment for services rendered in mind."

"Oh, no?"

"No." He stood, too, almost nose to nose with her. Dusty stiffened her spine to compensate for the slight advantage his height gave him.

"You needed help and I offered it. Given a chance, the attraction between us would follow its natural course. You, however, are too naive to recognize the message your body is sending."

His lips compressed into a thin, angry line, he picked up his jacket. Hooking a thumb into the collar, he slung the garment over his shoulder and strode toward the door. "Consider my offer rescinded. I have no time to waste on childish women."

The door slammed behind him.

"Childish?" Dusty echoed furiously. Grabbing an empty beer can, she flung it at the door. It opened.

Miguel leaned against the jamb, his gaze traveling from her to the can on the floor. "Before you throw your tantrum, I suggest you lock up. This isn't the best of neighborhoods." He closed the door, softly this time.

Dusty stared at the spot where he'd been standing, then crossed the room and slid the dead bolt into place. She didn't doubt that his anger was unfeigned. But was he angry because she'd seen through his seduction strategy or because she'd judged him unfairly?

No, he was a Romeo through and through. She returned to her bed and blew out the lantern. She wasn't going to fall into his trap. Calling her naive and childish was supposed to make her feel at fault and eager to show him how womanly she could be.

Well, it wouldn't work. She thumped her pillow for emphasis. But the memory of her reaction to the feathery touch of his lips rose unbidden in her mind and she flushed. She was attracted to Miguel . . . by more than a little.

Maybe she had overreacted. Slightly. She wasn't exactly experienced in these male-female games. And with Willys out of commission, she did need help. Should she apologize to him when she saw him on Tuesday?

She groaned. Apologies did not come easily to her. This was all her father's fault, she decided. If he'd just stuck to exploring Indian ruins in Canyonlands, she wouldn't be in this fix. Wouldn't be in Pinecreek at all.

But she was, and she was going to have to face Miguel again. In two days. Well, at least she'd have a reprieve until then.

MIGUEL PARKED in front of the converted Victorian house. Why he was wasting his time with an unwilling woman, he didn't know. Because of her he'd slept poorly and woken early. He couldn't forget the desolation he'd heard under the anger in Dusty's voice when she'd spoken of her missing father. She loved him. Miguel knew what it was like to love—and lose—a father.

She needed help and didn't know anyone else in town. Fearing he was getting in deeper than he'd intended, but unable to stop himself, he'd called his mechanic and arranged for her jeep to be taken to his garage. Then he'd gone straight to Carmen's and subjected himself to her gloating when she figured out that Dusty had denied him her bed.

Her husband, Juan, had been no more sympathetic. He'd willingly exchanged his four-wheel-drive Toyota truck for the sports car, but then insisted on relating the long history of his courtship of Carmen, and how he'd known she was the woman he wanted to marry.

When Miguel had finally extricated himself, he'd stopped at a bakery to buy sweet rolls and coffee as a peacemaking gesture. Proud, stubborn and independent though Dusty was, she needed him. He couldn't just walk away.

Besides, he didn't think she'd remain unwilling long.

ABOUT TO HIKE to La Margarita and check her jeep by the light of day, Dusty swung open the door as soon as she heard a knock.

"Don't you have enough sense to ask who it is or attach the safety chain before opening the door?" Miguel demanded.

"If I'd expected you, I wouldn't have answered it at all!" As the admission popped out of her mouth she realized that she'd been delaying her departure for the restaurant because she hadn't wanted to run into him.

He looked even better in snug, low-riding jeans than he did in his work clothes, she reluctantly noted. The knit of his pullover shirt clung to his broad shoulders and muscular chest. Its short sleeves confirmed her imagination's picture of nicely developed biceps. And the deep red hue emphasized his dusky skin and the sheen of his black hair.

Miguel grinned. "I come bearing gifts." He held up the bakery bag and cups of coffee. "May I come in?"

"I was on my way out to check on Willys."

"Willys is on the way to my mechanic's."

"I could have taken care of it."

"Did I say you couldn't? But when I woke up this morning, I thought, what better way to start the day than by rescuing a feminist in distress?" He chuckled. "Besides waking up next to her in bed, of course."

Dusty started slightly, half-afraid he knew what a starring role he'd played in her dreams, but he was only making light of their disagreement. Feeling both relieved and also tantalized by the aroma of the fresh coffee, she stepped back to allow him to enter. He crossed the room, set the bag and coffee cups upon the cooler and sat down on the floor, an act which assured her of his good intentions, but perversely left a trace of disappointment.

Following his example, she sat down on the bed and waited for an explanation.

"I think we were both tired last night," he said as he handed her one of the coffee cups, "and our tempers got away from us. Shall we consider ourselves forgiven and start over?"

Dusty smiled. Not only had he saved her from making a direct apology, he'd also saved himself. She nodded.

"Eat up," he added, opening the bag and handing her a sweet roll, "your four-wheel-drive chariot awaits." He paused. "No strings attached, except that I drive."

Dusty grabbed her coffee and took a big sip to aid the passage of the pride she knew she had to swallow. Then she ate half of a chocolate doughnut before she spoke. "You're very nice to help me."

"I am a gentleman even when in the company of a liberated lady." He polished off a cream puff and reached for another.

"Isn't that a contradiction in terms?"

"Liberated lady?" Miguel shook his head. "That depends on your definition of the terms."

"Liberated means thinking and acting for yourself. Not needing anyone. Independence versus dependence."

"And lady?"

His expression told her he was ready to pounce, but she plowed on. "A lady always speaks softly, sits with her ankles crossed, wears dresses and minces instead of walks because she's got on high heels."

"If you say so." Miguel dropped their empty cups into the bakery bag and crumpled it. "Let's get going."

Dusty gaped at him. "You mean you agree with me?"

"Hardly." He took her by the hand and pulled her to her feet. "But I have a feeling we could argue about this all day."

His hand was smooth while hers was rough, callused from a summer of rock climbing. Uncomfortably aware of the difference, Dusty slipped her hand free and picked up her knapsack. It was, she knew, supposed to be the other way around.

But she persisted. "What's your definition of a lady?" she asked, following him out, then stopping to lock the door.

"A woman who enjoys her femininity."

"That leaves me out." Dusty hurried to catch up with him as he reached the end of the hall and descended the stairs.

"Why?" He opened the front door for her and she sailed past without answering. How could she explain how she'd felt limited by her sex from the day her father had told her that a girl's place was with her mother?

"Thank you," he said pointedly as he joined her on the sidewalk leading to the street.

"I didn't ask you to hold open the door."

"But I did it out of courtesy. Can't a liberated lady—woman—be polite in return?"

"It all seems like a lot of outdated rigmarole to me."

"Guess I'm an old-fashioned guy."

"But I'm not an old-fashioned female who needs a man to take care of her."

"Of course," Miguel said. They reached the curb, where a red Toyota pickup truck waited. A sign painted on the door announced Juan's Landscaping Service. "That's why the only thing that beats rescuing a feminist in distress is waking up—"

"How is Juan going to use your Miata for work?" Dusty interrupted hastily.

"This is his personal truck. The sign is advertising." Miguel opened the passenger door, Dusty climbed in and fastened her seat belt. When he stood waiting, she turned to him.

"Thank you," she said with affected sweetness.

"You're welcome." Miguel was all sincerity and Dusty rolled her eyes. About to give him directions when he slid behind the steering wheel and slipped into his seat belt, she realized she'd left her map in the jeep. They swung by the garage to get it and to drop off her key, then headed out of town.

The paved roads lined with stately old homes and sweeping lawns gave way to gravel and forest. The scent of pine drifted in the open windows, sunlight filtered through the treetops to dapple the shaded ground, a squirrel chittered and a raven cawed an answer.

"If you define independence as not needing anyone, isn't that lonely?" Miguel asked suddenly.

"You don't have to need someone to enjoy company."

"You admit that you do need company?"

Dusty eyed him suspiciously. "What's your point?"

Miguel grinned. "Not in the mood for fencing today?"

"I can't fence if I don't know what you're getting at."

"Your sarcasm betrays your discomfort." He glanced at her smugly, then turned his attention back to the bumpy road. "Everyone—male or female—needs people. Accepting my help does not weaken you or make you dependent on me."

"Well, that's good to hear."

"Does that mean you'll concede to my definition of liberated?"

Dusty squirmed in her seat; he'd picked up the thread of their earlier debate. "Be more exact."

"Liberated, as you said, means the ability to act and think for oneself, but, I'd add, within the framework of others. An interdependency rather than independence. I help you today, you help me another day."

"Just how am I supposed to help you?"

Miguel grinned. "Suspicious little lady, aren't you?"

"I'm neither little nor a lady."

"You're smaller than I am and you're a sexy, feminine woman, although you choose to deny it. I'm curious why. Don't you like men?"

"I just don't believe in turning into a simpering, helpless idiot in the presence of a sexy package of male muscle."

"Are you speaking of me?"

"You're not bad." Dusty kept her tone bland, but didn't dare look at him.

"And if you admitted you were attracted to me, you'd feel you were at a disadvantage?"

"Want to arm wrestle?" She faced him, her chin lifted in challenge.

Miguel met her glance, his dark eyes dancing with mischief. "Leg wrestling would be more fun." His gaze swept over her long, bare legs before returning to the road.

The image of her legs entwined with his stole Dusty's breath and she didn't answer.

Miguel reached out and circled her bicep with his hand. His fingers met. "Mine is bigger than yours." Puffing out his chest, he took his right hand from the wheel and flexed his arm. Dusty squeezed his bicep. Easily twice the size of hers, it felt like steel beneath warm flesh.

"A mere marshmallow," she said with mock disdain.

"Biologically, you have to admit I'm stronger than you are. Why do you want to deny the difference between the sexes? They complement one another. Men need women and women need men. Why are you afraid of that?"

Dusty bristled. "I'm not afraid. I think I could beat you. Arm wrestling has as much to do with technique and concentration as strength."

"You're avoiding my question."

"You're avoiding mine."

"Lady, you're on for a match. What's the prize?"

"Ten bucks?"

"No way! How about a kiss?"

"On the cheek?"

Miguel stopped the truck in the middle of the road and turned in his seat to face her. "I was thinking more of a long—" he drew out his words "—slow . . . wet . . . meeting of the mouths."

"Oh." Dusty couldn't think of anything else to say; her eyes insisted on focusing on the tiny depression above the dip in his upper lip. She repressed a moan, unable to deny that she wanted his kiss . . . unable to deny that she was afraid of the power of her desire.

"What prize will you claim if you win?" His voice, soft, but deep, coursed through her like a river. Her breasts seemed to swell, as if longing to press against his male, flat chest, and the muscles at the apex of her thighs to contract, as if begging to have that emptiness filled.

Her gaze drifted upward, lingering over the shadow of beard on his cheeks as she imagined them bristled and scraping against her skin, then rose higher to meet his eyes. His eyelids were heavy, his pupils dark yet lit with an inner warmth that shot an answering heat all the way to her toes.

"The same," Dusty admitted in a voice so throaty she barely recognized it as her own. She heard Miguel suck in his breath. He swallowed and she watched the movement of his Adam's apple. *How would it feel beneath her lips?*

"Well, then—" his voice was throaty, too "—it looks like neither of us can lose." His smile was slow and sensual now, full of secret promise.

Then he put the truck back into gear and drove on.

What was he doing? Dusty fumed. She'd practically offered herself on a silver platter, he'd said "Fine," then returned to his driving!

She was out of her depth. She didn't know diddly about dating or mating. Longing to be with her father and fighting her mother's efforts to instill femininity and domesticity into her, Dusty had deliberately scorned the coy, male-female games of adolescence. Her experience consisted of one short-term affair.

The summer after her high school graduation, working among the older, more worldly guides on the Colorado River raft trips, she'd been embarrassed by her virginity. So she'd welcomed the overtures of a tourist not much older—or experienced—than her. Chad had been kind, sweet and awkward. She hadn't minded when his vacation ended and he returned to the East Coast, nor had she been tempted to repeat the experience—until now.

"Here's Horseshoe Bend," Miguel said, breaking into her thoughts and coming to a stop. "Where did you say we go from here?"

Dusty glanced at the wood frame general store with hitching posts and gas pumps in front. "People live out here?" she asked, adopting his casual tone and pulling out her map.

"Mostly summer people from Phoenix." Miguel pointed toward a group of fancy log cabins tucked back among the trees. "I'm going in to get a soda. Want anything?"

"A cola, please." She buried her nose in the map and he went into the store.

MIGUEL SMILED at the woman behind the counter and returned her pleasant greeting, then headed straight through the narrow, crowded aisles to the refrigerator section. Opening one of the glass doors, he stood in front of the chilled air, substituting it for the cold shower he needed. In lieu of shoving the sodas aside and climbing in, he rested his forehead on one shelf.

The look in Dusty's eyes when she'd said she wanted a kiss if she lost the arm wrestling match had set him on fire—not to mention the lower lip that had seemed to pout in invitation. If he'd had to stay in the small cab of the truck with her a second longer, he would have jumped her then and there.

He should, he thought with amusement, raising his head and pretending to study the sodas, buy a bag of ice and carry it in his lap. He'd wanted other women before, but not like Dusty. She was an entrancing mix of strength and vulnerability and the feelings she aroused frightened him.

Only fools rushed in where angels feared to tread. And he was neither. With Dusty, he was going to take things nice and slow. One step at a time. Mona's warning that he might wind up bringing Dusty her slippers echoed in his mind.

Grabbing several cans of soda and some sandwiches, he returned to the counter. He bought a bag of ice, too, then dumped his purchases into the cooler in the back of the truck.

"Diet?" Dusty asked as he handed her a soda after climbing back behind the steering wheel. "Your mother wants me to gain weight and you want me to lose it?"

Miguel looked at the can in his hand. It, too, was diet. He hated the aftertaste of artificial sweeteners. He opened it and took a huge gulp. "Sugar's bad for you. I drink diet all the time. Want me to take yours back?"

"I'll do it. I should ask if anyone has seen my father." She jumped out of the truck and ran into the store. Miguel pressed the cool can against his forehead and watched her tight, rounded buttocks and long, tanned legs climb the stairs into the store. The view from the front when she returned was even worse. Her breasts, unfettered beneath the baggy T-shirt, bounced and swayed with her rapid movements.

"Any luck?" he asked, when she climbed in and popped open her soda.

She nodded. "He's been in for supplies, but not for several weeks." Worry creased her smooth forehead and guilt pushed Miguel's sexual attraction aside. He'd completely forgotten the search they were conducting.

"Where do we go from here?" he asked, figuring progress would ease her anxiety.

"Continue straight and watch for Forest Road 163. It could be bad if it's like any of the ones I've been on lately. Want me to drive?"

"Are you questioning my ability?" His ego piqued, Miguel cast her a dark look of warning.

"Not ability but experience," she assured him. "Four-wheeling is quite different than driving a sports car over paved highways."

"I think I can manage."

"Seat belts," Dusty commanded, fastening her own; Miguel followed suit.

When they reached the road, Miguel put the truck into four-wheel and swore the angle of ascent was a straight ninety degrees. He took it slowly but steadily, knowing that if he faltered, they could get stuck in a rut. Dusty praised him mightily when he reached the top and he couldn't help beaming with what he felt was ridiculous pleasure.

"Keep an eye out for a black Ford pickup with a homemade, wooden camper," Dusty told him as the road leveled out. "He'd camp off the road, so go slowly and check out any path wide enough for us, especially if there's water."

Miguel slowed to a crawl. Many of the side paths they found were dead ends without enough room to turn around, so he had to back up repeatedly. He stopped at every overlook and allowed Dusty to scan the canyons with her binoculars. The process was tedious and slow and he quickly understood her frustration with both her father and the search.

They talked to pass the time. When Dusty decided to play "Twenty Questions" about his life, Miguel answered willingly. His father, he explained, had moved up from Phoenix and opened La Margarita when he was twenty-five. His mother had worked as a bus girl. Although she was only seventeen, it was a case of love at first sight and they were married on her eighteenth birthday. Miguel was born ten months later, Carmen after two years, Luisa two years after that and Ramona five years after Luisa.

"I was ten and Mona barely a year when Papá was killed," he concluded. "He'd gone to Phoenix to try to get a loan to expand the restaurant. The tourists and retirees had discovered Pinecreek and business was growing." He shook his head. "He was stopped at a traffic light. The brakes on a truck coming up behind him failed and the collision pushed him into an on-coming car. He died instantly."

"I'm sorry."

Miguel nodded his acceptance of her sympathy. "He was a good man. Maybe not quite the saint Mamá has made him, but he loved her and he loved us. He worked hard, and what material things he couldn't give us, he made up for with his attention."

He caught sight of a sunlit meadow tucked behind some trees and paused. "Let's stop for lunch," he suggested. "It's after two and I could stretch my legs." Searching for a place to pull off the road, he found a rutted path beside a small brook, but when it veered away from the meadow, he stopped.

"Let's walk the rest of the way in. I don't want to end up in Timbuktu."

"Can't we eat and drive?" Dusty asked. "This looks promising. Dad would camp near water."

Miguel shook his head and pulled the key from the ignition. "Our food will digest better if our stomachs aren't bouncing up and down." He climbed out of the truck and walked to the passenger side. "We'll take this road to the end after we eat." He opened the door, released her seat belt and lifted her out before she could protest. She stared at him with startled eyes and parted lips, apparently not expecting him to move her so easily.

"Light as a feather," he told her, grinning at her surprise. Setting her down, he felt his grin fade; he was standing close enough to her to feel the gentle rise and fall of her breasts against his chest.

Not now, he told the stirrings in his groin. He moved to the back of the open truck and reached in. He tossed Dusty a blanket, pulled out the cooler and headed through the trees to the meadow. She caught up with him as he set the cooler down and spread the blanket.

"Mamá had always helped in the restaurant," Miguel continued. He had to keep his mind off the temptation to push Dusty back onto the blanket and cover her body with his. When they made love, he wanted to take his time.

"And she took it over. Her family wanted her to move home with them, but she wouldn't sell the restaurant that had been so much a part of my father." He opened the cooler and handed Dusty a sandwich, then took one for himself.

"She worked eighteen-hour days and kept Mona in a playpen in the kitchen until the rest of us got home from school. She was strong for us, but I heard her cry herself to sleep at night. She tried to hide the sound with her pillow, but I listened and I heard."

He bit into his sandwich. "I was the man of the family. That's what everyone told me at the funeral," he added after he swallowed. "But I was ten years old. What could I do?"

He didn't hide his bitterness. Dusty had been honest with him about her family and he saw no reason to hide his feelings. She munched on her roast beef sandwich, but her brown eyes were fixed on him.

"I couldn't do much to help Mamá with money, but I could take care of the girls, and the three of us cleaned house as best we could." He grinned. "I even learned how to change Mona's diapers! I remind her of that whenever I want to get her goat."

Dusty smiled as he'd meant her to. "You're still a very close family, aren't you?" she said and he thought he heard a hint of wistfulness in her voice.

He nodded. "Although I've been accused of being bossy at times."

"No!" Dusty exclaimed in feigned astonishment, then burst into laughter.

Miguel grinned again. "Carmen swore no guy ever asked her for a second date after the inquisition I put him through. She and Luisa begged Mamá to send me away to college. She agreed with them, said it was time for me to have a life of my own. I respect her for that."

Dusty nodded her agreement. They ate in silence for a while, then she spoke. "Is that why you're helping me? Like your sisters, I bring out your protective instincts?"

Miguel put down his sandwich and studied her intently. "Believe me, Dusty," he said without a smile, "when I say I feel anything but brotherly toward you."

He watched her swallow a mouthful of sandwich and lay down the rest of it. Her gaze wavered with the hint of shyness that intrigued him, then slowly rose to meet and lock with his. He leaned toward her, but in his peripherel vision saw something move behind her.

"Hold still," he warned abruptly, reaching for a rock without taking his eyes off the coyote creeping toward them through the tall grass. It must be rabid, he thought, to approach them in broad daylight. "Be ready to run to the closest tree," he told Dusty. He closed his hand over a good-sized stone. She turned as he raised his arm.

"Don't!" she cried, knocking the rock from his grasp. "It's Cody, my father's dog!"

5

"ARE YOU SURE?" Miguel grabbed for another stone as the animal slunk down and disappeared into the tall grass.

"Cody, it's me!" Dusty rose to her knees and clapped her hands. "C'mon, boy!"

The dog hurtled forward with an excited yelp. Hugging him to her chest, Dusty rolled back onto the blanket. Miguel tossed the rock aside and grabbed the remains of their sandwiches.

"Cody, meet Miguel," Dusty said. The dog licked her cheek, then sat up and extended one paw, tail thumping the ground behind him. "Mangiest mutt in the West," she said proudly, as Miguel gingerly shook hands with the dog. "Did you think he was a coyote?"

He nodded. "You're about a quarter to half right," she added, "but the rest is a mystery." She laughed and rubbed the dog's ears, but his attention was clearly on the food laying on the blanket beside Miguel. "Let him have the meat from my sandwich," she said. "Dad spoils him terribly, and he'll beg until you feed him."

"Where's your master, eh?" Miguel asked, giving the dog small bites of roast beef.

"His camp must be nearby," Dusty answered as she stood. "Cody usually sticks to him like glue." She shaded her eyes and peered into the shadows of the trees around the meadow. "Maybe it's up the road a little more."

Turning back to Miguel, she saw him feed the dog the turkey from his sandwich, then recoil when Cody tried to lick his face in gratitude. Despite the rejection, the dog curled up next to him, his head in Miguel's lap. Taking a closer look at Cody, Dusty noticed his coat was matted and full of burrs. He was thinner than she remembered, and it wasn't like him to settle down like that. Normally he danced around her, dashing off to bring sticks for her to throw and begging her to play.

"Something's wrong with him," she said, kneeling by the dog. Cody yawned and snuggled even closer to Miguel, whose dark eyes reflected her own concern. She stroked Cody and felt the ridges of his ribs clearly defined beneath the matted fur.

"Want to take the truck or walk up the road?" Miguel asked.

"The truck." They both stood and Cody struggled to his feet. "He's half-starved and exhausted," Dusty said. "Dad wouldn't neglect him like this."

What had happened to her father? Had he fallen into an abandoned mine? Slipped off a cliff, broken a leg and sent Cody for help? Been bitten by a rattlesnake? All the reasons not to hike in the backcountry alone reverberated in her head—reasons both she and her father had scoffed at, believing they only applied to the inexperienced. She blinked rapidly and tried to swallow the waves of dread and panic rising in her throat.

Miguel pulled her into his arms and hugged her. "Cody probably chased a rabbit and got lost," he said. "Let's get him to the truck and look around."

Dusty held on to him, hiding her face in his shoulder. What Miguel didn't know was that Cody rarely wandered from her father's side and Jack, equally devoted, would never willingly abandon his dog. But his suggestion offered a strand of hope and she clung to it. Realizing she was also clinging to Miguel's strong body, she stepped out of his embrace and summoned a tremulous smile, silently thanking him for his gentle reassurance.

"We'll find him," he said, his voice quiet but determined. He brushed her cheek with his fingertips, then picked up the dog and carried him to the truck.

Once past the meadow, the trail into the forest narrowed and widened, twisted and turned, following the course of the small stream and taking them higher into the mountains. The farther away from the meadow they got, the more Dusty's worry mounted. Then they rounded a bend, where the trees on each side of the trail thinned, and they entered a canyon lined with sheer stone walls. Water trickled down the opposite side and landed in a pool beneath a thick grove of cottonwood trees. Leaves turning gold in the autumnal air shone in the sun, but it was the glint of black metal beneath their canopy that made Dusty cry out with relief.

Cody sat up and sniffed the air, then barked. Miguel pressed the accelerator and hurried the truck along the smooth surface of the path through the canyon. Cody's yips grew in volume as they neared the cottonwood grove. Miguel stopped and Dusty opened the door. Cody jumped over her lap and she scrambled out behind him.

"It's Dad's truck!" she cried, recognizing the battered Ford and running forward. She called, but her father did not appear. "Dad?" she finished weakly and looked around.

A hammock, twisted by the wind, hung between two trees. A small charcoal grill, overturned, lay by a blackened ring of stones. A folding camp stool, collapsed and torn, sprawled on the ground a few feet away. A propane lantern sat amid the glass shards of its globe at the base of a large, flat rock. A fishing pole, broken in two, poked out of the shrubs by the pond.

Cody sniffed around the camp, then sat abruptly and lifted his nose to the sky. And howled. A long, plaintive howl that tore at her heart.

"Maybe he's out looking for Cody," Miguel suggested, laying a comforting hand upon her shoulder.

"I don't think so." Dusty tried to speak quietly, fighting the scream lurking in her throat that wanted to answer Cody's howl. The camp was deserted, abandoned. She moved to kneel beside the dog and wrapped her arms around him. "You're not lost, are you?" she told him. "It's Jack who's lost." Cody's howls faded into a low whine as she comforted him.

She felt Miguel's presence beside her. His silence, she guessed, meant he agreed with her. Unable to look at him and have her fear confirmed by a sympathetic expression on his face, she rose and moved to the back of the truck.

An empty dog food bag, torn to shreds, lay in the middle of the floor. Cody's work, she guessed, watching the dog jump into the truck and nose at the remnants of the bag. He'd probably hung around the camp as long as the food held out, then hunger had driven him away. But the dog wasn't capable of breaking open the locks on the cabinets built into the sides of the camper. Clothes, pots and pans, tools, soap, towels—all her father's meager possessions lay scattered about.

"Don't touch anything." Miguel's hand on her arm restrained her as she lifted one foot to follow Cody into the truck. "We should notify the police," he persisted, tightening his grip when she tried to pull free.

"They wouldn't know what's missing," she snapped, her temper rising. Why was he interfering?

"What about fingerprints?" he argued, maintaining a maddening calm. "I hate to say this, but from the looks of things, foul play might be involved. You could ruin valuable evidence."

Dusty sighed, still irritated. But he was right. "I don't see his backpack or bedroll," she said. "Maybe Cody got lost chasing a rabbit, like you said, and Dad's searching for him." She was grasping at straws, she knew, but she couldn't let herself think that anything had harmed her father.

"If your dad was going to be gone overnight, would he leave his camper open?"

Seeing the sympathy in his dark eyes, Dusty looked away and kicked at the ground with one sneakered foot. Her frustration rose as Miguel's arguments were forcing her to face what she already knew. Jack would have cleaned up his camp and stowed his belongings in the truck. And he would've taken his fishing pole with him.

"Someone could have broken into his truck while he was away."

"All the more reason not to touch anything. Wouldn't your father want the thieves caught?"

"Yes." She gave the ransacked interior of the camper one last, longing look and turned away. "Let's see if we can find anything else." She heard Cody bark, then felt him close on her heels.

When they found a pickax and gold panning equipment as well as something Miguel called a drywasher by the pond, Dusty sank to the ground in relief. Cody curled up by her side. "At least he's not at the bottom of a mine," she said, freed of one fear when Miguel explained how the drywasher was used to separate gold from the soil.

"There aren't any deep mines in the area," he assured her, sitting down on the other side of Cody. "An old guy who owns a placer claim comes into the restaurant and eats at the bar. He's told me more than I ever wanted to know about mining." He stood and offered her his hand. "Let's go back to town and report this to the police. They can organize a search-and-rescue team."

Dusty hugged her knees to her chest and chewed her lip. "Do you think they'd do that?"

"Why not?"

"He lives out of his truck. They'll think he's a bum."

"He's a human being and he's missing. What he does or where he lives doesn't matter." At that Dusty took his hand and, as he pulled her to her feet, she hugged him impulsively.

"Thank you," she said.

"For what?" Miguel's arms tightened around her when she tried to step back.

"For helping me." She gazed into his dark eyes. "For being here. I'm glad I'm not alone." The admission didn't come easily to her, but she felt she owed him an apology. Restaurant Romeo or not, she could no longer doubt that his help was freely given.

"You're welcome." His smile was gentle, caring and infinitely sweet. "I'm glad, too." He pulled her closer.

Dusty relaxed against him, not fighting the warmth, security and strength she felt in his embrace. She'd always thought such sentiments would weaken her, but somehow, this time, they made her feel stronger. Accepting rather than questioning that strength, she squeezed Miguel's waist, then stepped back.

"Ready to go?" he asked and she nodded.

Her fear and panic had receded. Worry remained, but her father was no novice to the backcountry. He might be hurt, but he could keep himself alive until she found him. He had to.

"WHAT WAS YOUR FATHER doing in the mountains, and how long has he been missing?" Bob Kelly, the balding sergeant in the county sheriff's department wanted to know.

"At least three weeks," Dusty answered and explained that Jack had moved to the area in the spring in the hope of exercising his right under the 1872 Mining Law to mine any profitable ore he found on public land. The last time she'd heard from him had been in mid-August, when he'd written to confirm his plan to join her on the first of September. As she talked, she felt

Miguel's hand take hers in a warm, reassuring grip. They sat together, facing Sergeant Kelly's desk.

"I know he wouldn't abandon his dog," she insisted, seeing the sergeant's skeptical expression. "And if he'd gone hiking, he would have stowed his camping equipment in his truck and locked it. I don't know what could have happened to him, but I know he's missing. Please . . ." She paused and blinked back the tears she could feel gathering in her eyes. "Please, will you look for him?"

The sergeant's face softened. "Of course we'll look for him. I have to ask you all these questions to get an idea of how far he could have gone and where to look." He glanced at Miguel, then back at Dusty. "I have to warn you, though," he said, his voice kind for the first time since they'd entered his office, "that not many people can survive alone in the wilderness for more than a few days."

"My dad could." Dusty met his steady gaze fiercely, willing him to believe her. "He has his backpack and bedroll."

He nodded, then rose to his feet and held out his hand. "We'll do everything we can to find him." He glanced at his watch. "It's too close to dark to go out now, but we'll start at dawn. Try not to worry in the meantime."

Thanking him, Dusty and Miguel left. *Hang on for one more night, Dad,* Dusty prayed silently as they returned to the truck, and headed for a veterinarian's office.

"NEXT STOP, the grocery store," Miguel said after the vet had examined Cody and pronounced him healthy, but weakened. A few days of rest and good food and he'd be back to normal. "What would you like for dinner?"

"Me?" Dusty asked, startled. "I have sandwich makings at home. I only need to get dog food."

"You don't think I'm going to drop you off and leave you to stare at four walls and worry, do you?"

"You've done so much already," Dusty felt obliged to tell him, "and I'm afraid I won't be much company."

"Conversation not required," he assured her. "We'll give Cody a bath, have some dinner and watch television."

"Really, I'll be fine at home."

Miguel pulled into the grocery store parking lot. "You're coming home with me," he said, resting one arm on the steering wheel and turning toward her. "If for no other reason than that I have a fenced yard for the dog. I won't take no for an answer."

"Your brotherly bossiness is showing."

"Does that mean yes?"

Dusty studied him for a moment. His hair had escaped its careful styling, and the shadow of his beard had darkened into bristles. He looked deliciously male.

"Yes," she answered.

MIGUEL LIVED HALFWAY up Tabletop, the highest mountain overlooking Pinecreek. Most of the houses Dusty glimpsed among the tall pines were large and modern, constructed of natural wood and glass. But

Miguel's, at the end of a shady gravel lane beyond the paved road, was small, old and unpretentious.

A smaller version of the Victorian mansions built in town by early settlers, it was painted a pearly gray, its trim done in shades of a darker gray and burgundy. The colors blended nicely with the boulder-strewn and pine-dotted landscape, Dusty thought and told him so.

"Thank you," he said simply, but pride touched his face. He parked the truck in front of a matching garage. "I've put a lot of work into it." He climbed out and pulled their grocery bags from the back.

Not waiting for him to reach her door, Dusty got out and held it for Cody.

"Of course, if I'd known what I was doing, it wouldn't have taken as long," he added as she closed the door and he joined her. "I learned as I went and a couple of times I had to hire someone to fix my mistakes." He led them to a gate in a white picket fence and ushered them into the backyard.

"You're a gardener?" Dusty couldn't keep the amazement from her voice at the sight of raised beds bordered by old railroad ties and filled with vegetables, herbs and flowers.

"Mamá said I always liked to play in the dirt," he said with a cheerful grin. "The tomatoes and peppers have about had it, but you have your choice of broccoli, peas, carrots or cauliflower with your hamburger."

"Do we have to shell the peas?"

"No, they're snow peas."

"All four," Dusty said.

"Indecisive, are you?" His smile teased her.

She shook her head and followed him toward the back door. "I love fresh vegetables."

"We'll have a vegetable medley, then." He eyed Cody, who had joined them on the doorstep. "But first, a bath for this mangy mutt before he gets the run of the house."

They entered the kitchen. "We could leave him in the yard," Dusty suggested halfheartedly. The dog's presence helped to fill the aching hole in her heart, but it wasn't her house.

Miguel set the grocery bags upon the counter, put their ground beef into the refrigerator, then pulled the dog dishes they'd bought out of the bags. "I think he'd rather be with us, don't you?" He filled one of the bowls with water and set it upon the floor by the door. "Should we feed him more now or wait until after his bath?"

"After." Surprised by the sting of tears, Dusty bowed her head and blinked rapidly as she set out the dog food. Although pleased with Miguel's thoughtfulness and relieved that she didn't have to part with the dog, she had to admit that worry over her father's disappearance had wreaked havoc with her emotions.

Taking a deep breath to regain control, she lifted her head and smiled. "It'll be his reward, because he might not enjoy his bath," she added.

Miguel straightened and looked at her worriedly, while Cody lapped at the water. "Will he bite?"

"Not too hard." Dusty did her best, but couldn't keep a straight face.

"For that—" Miguel waved an admonishing finger "—you can comb him while I get towels." He handed her the metal comb and dog shampoo they'd purchased. "You get to the basement through here," he said, moving into a hallway off the kitchen and opening a door.

He continued down the hall, but she stopped to peek into the living room. A large picture window framed a wide view of the town in the valley below them. Stereo components filled a bookcase and speakers flanked a stone fireplace. The furniture was plain but looked comfortable. Big throw pillows in front of the fireplace and smaller ones on the couch and easy chairs splashed the room with color. Potted palms and hanging spider plants provided a cool, green contrast.

Cozy, she thought. She led Cody down the stairs to the basement and began combing him. Not at all the bachelor pad she'd expected. And he'd renovated it himself. Only his sports car fitted the image of the playboy she'd believed him to be. And his car, she had to admit, would be fun to drive.

She couldn't she realized have been more wrong about him.

6

MIGUEL PASSED THROUGH his bedroom and entered the adjoining bath. Pulling towels from the linen closet, he told himself to keep his mind on Cody. Although Dusty seemed certain that her father was alive, her emotions simmered very close to the surface. Such vulnerability and her gratitude made her easy prey for a seduction. But that wasn't what he wanted. She was proud and independent and had to desire him as much as he desired her.

Anything less, he sensed, spelled danger. To win his way into her arms without her total capitulation would be tantamount to losing. A one-sided affair would give her too much power over him. He'd wind up, as Mona had warned, literally bringing Dusty her slippers.

For now he'd be the friend she needed and no more. A decision more easily made than executed he realized when he joined her in the basement and she looked up from combing Cody to smile at him. That smile was the warmest he'd received from her, and it was all he could do not to cross the room and claim those full lips. Instead he dropped the towels onto a counter and ran water into the laundry tubs.

"That's about the best I can do," Dusty said, sitting back and laying down the comb. "We can use our fingers to untangle the rest of the snarls while we wash him."

Miguel advanced on the dog, but Cody backed up. "C'mon boy," he crooned, "let's get nice and clean, then we'll cook you a juicy burger to eat with your dry, boring food."

Cody cocked his head and lifted his ears at Miguel's soft words, but continued to retreat a step for each one of Miguel's. "I don't think he's buying it," Dusty said in a low voice, joining the advance. When they'd backed him into a corner, Miguel swooped down and slipped his arms beneath Cody's belly. Rising, he took him straight to the large sinks and set him gently into the warm water.

"Is it too hot?" he asked Dusty.

She checked the temperature and shook her head, then used one hand to scoop water onto the dog's back, while she helped hold him in place with the other. Miguel grabbed a plastic bowl from a shelf and helped her wet him down. Cody bore their ministrations with a pained but patient air.

When he was thoroughly wet and bedraggled, Cody shook himself vigorously, soaking both of his bathers. "Wait until we're done!" Dusty yelled, but laughed at Miguel's offended expression. "You didn't think we could do this and stay dry, did you?" she asked.

"I've never washed a dog before," Miguel muttered, struggling unsuccessfully to keep his gaze on the dog. The thin cotton of Dusty's wet T-shirt clung provocatively to her breasts. His hands curled into empty fists and rested on Cody's back as he forgot about the dog, forgot about everything but the urge to cup those soft mounds and bring them to his mouth.

Still laughing, and unaware of her revealing T-shirt, Dusty reached across the sink for the shampoo. Slipping free, Cody leaped over the edge of the tub and took off.

"Oh, no!" Dusty scrambled after him, but Cody evaded her. Miguel was slower to turn from the tub, slower yet to move. He stood and stared while Dusty ran around the room after the dog. Through the pale yellow of the wet cotton plastered against her flesh, he could see that her swaying breasts were a lighter shade than the rest of her tanned skin, could see the rosy pink of the areolas circling her nipples. Heat gathered in his loins.

"Are you going to help or just stand there and watch?" Dusty yelled indignantly, turning her back upon him. Cody took refuge behind a pillar separating the unfinished laundry area from the carpeted floor where a pool table reigned. When she feinted left, the dog moved right and vice versa.

The view from the back wasn't bad, either, Miguel decided, moving forward reluctantly. She had a small waist and nicely rounded hips, not to mention long, tightly muscled, shapely legs.

"We'll do a first-class football tackle," he told her. "You work from the left of the post and I'll take the right." He hunkered down on his heels and Dusty followed suit. Cody perked up his ears and cocked his head to one side, as he watched this new development.

"You move first and he'll head toward the pool table, where I'll trap him." Miguel whispered his strategy as if Cody could hear and understand them.

Dusty nodded her agreement, then mouthed the words, "One, two, three . . ."

She hurtled around the post, Cody darted to the right, Miguel threw himself forward . . . and tackled Dusty. His momentum propelled her onto her back and he landed on top of her. Cody disappeared beneath the pool table.

Her breath came out in a whoosh and she looked up at him with wide, startled eyes and parted lips. He stared down at her, intensely aware of the softness cushioning his chest, of the warmth of their flesh seeping through the wet fabric of their shirts.

"Are you all right?" he asked, lifting himself slightly, but unable to bring himself to roll off her completely. He would, he assured himself . . . in a minute.

She smiled and raised her hands to rest them lightly on his shoulders. "Great tackle," she said, her brown eyes sparkling with laughter.

"I didn't think he'd fit under the pool table." Miguel grinned back at her, then watched her smile fade as her gaze drifted to his lips.

"Aw, hell," he muttered and tossed aside his tenuous restraint.

At last Dusty thought wrapping her arms around Miguel's neck welcoming his hard, deep kiss. Her body felt as hot as molten lava, fluid beneath his weight, yielding and yearning for his touch everywhere at once.

His tongue flicked against her lips and hers darted forward to dance with his.

He rolled over and she moved with him, instinctively sliding one leg over his to keep their bodies together. His left arm cradled her head, while his free hand glided down the dip of her waist and up the slope of her hip, traveling the same route several times before he settled his palm on the sensitive skin next to her breast and splayed his fingers on her back. Rotating his fingertips, he encouraged her to rub her breasts against the hard wall of his chest. The sensation filled her with pleasure, but the barrier of their clothes tormented her, preventing the touch of flesh against flesh.

She lowered her hands to his shoulder blades, massaging them in rhythm with her writhing to intensify the erotic yet frustrating friction. But it wasn't enough, not close to what her senses demanded. Moaning she dropped her hands to his waist to yank up his shirt.

In a smooth motion, Miguel pushed up hers and cupped her bare breasts. Dusty cried out in release, raised her arms above her head and arched her back, thrusting her swollen fullness into his hands. Her nipples felt as rigid as spear points, yet the sensitive peaks rolled beneath his palms, and she shuddered with pleasure.

He nudged her to her back and straddled her, his fingers alternately kneading her pliant softness, then tracing the rosy circles of her areolas, before thumbing the stiff points at their centers. Dusty twisted and turned, the fleeting fulfillment she'd felt at the touch of his hands upon her bare breasts transformed into a deeper yearning that made her pull him down atop her.

Miguel lowered himself willingly circling her head with his arms and weaving his fingers into the silky strands of her hair. His lips covered hers and his bare chest replaced the warmth of his hands on her breasts. She caressed the muscles and sinews of his back with hard strokes of her hands, letting her hips and tongue respond to the rhythms of his.

Then something cold, spongy and slightly moist pressed against the side of her throat and a curious, snuffling noise intruded upon her consciousness. Miguel heard it, too; his rhythmic motion faltered, then stopped. She felt him lift his head and move his arm, as if brushing something away.

It didn't go away. The snuffling turned into a whine and she opened her eyes. "Cody!" Encouraged by her recognition the dog wormed his head beneath Miguel and across her collarbone.

"Ugh." She heard Miguel's protest but couldn't see him over Cody and felt his weight lift. "You're still wet. It's back to the tub for you." He stood, taking the dog with him. Cody lifted his head to Miguel's shoulder and stared at her with mournful eyes.

"Don't expect any pity from me," she told him, sitting up and pulling her T-shirt down over her breasts. The shirt was now dry, she noticed, which didn't surprise her, considering the heat of desire still pulsing within her, an unsatisfied ache slowly growing quiescent as she returned to reality.

The dog whined plaintively. "Don't complain because the water's cold," she heard Miguel say. "It's your own fault."

She knew she should get up and help him, but chose instead to stare at his back. He'd taken off his shirt. The smooth skin she still longed to caress rippled over muscle while he scrubbed the dog.

She wanted him.

But she didn't want to.

Tearing her gaze away, she bent her legs and wrapped her arms around them, then propped her chin on her knees. Books and movies glorified passion, but she neither read nor believed such fiction. From what she'd seen of life, passion clouded the brains of otherwise intelligent people and led them to making stupid mistakes. Her parents' marriage had been a prime example.

Not that she hadn't seen good relationships. Her mother was as happy with Fred as she'd been unhappy with Jack. Couples in Moab lived and worked with one another harmoniously.

Common interests seemed to be the key. Without them, painful disappointment followed. She shuddered, thinking of her self-appointed "big brother," Wayne Landis. He'd grown up in Moab, worked as a river runner, then left in his mid-twenties to go to college. He'd returned with a degree in archaeology, a job with the Bureau of Land Management—and a wife, Rachel.

Rachel had tried to adjust to Wayne's life in Moab. But small and delicate, she tired easily and couldn't keep up or carry her weight on backpacking trips. Rapids on raft trips and rock climbing terrified her. Unable to share the interests of Wayne's friends, she'd grown to resent them, considering them competitors for her husband's time and attention.

Coming from a large, close family, she'd believed Wayne should spend his free time with her. So he'd gradually given up his outdoor activities, to spend his weekends working on their home, visiting Rachel's family in Salt Lake City or entertaining them when they visited Moab.

But he hadn't been able to resist a raft trip with friends down Cataract Canyon, well-known for rapids rated up to Class 5 in difficulty. He'd begged Rachel to understand that he couldn't give such trips up completely but on his return he'd found an empty house and a note.

Passion had brought Wayne and Rachel together, but hadn't been able to overcome their differences.

And that was all that she and Miguel shared. It was an attraction of opposites. His attitude toward women was too traditional for her and she was too independent for him.

Wishing she could rid herself of her unwanted and unsatisfied desire by shaking herself as vigorously as Cody had done, Dusty jumped to her feet and went to help Miguel wash the dog.

"Okay, Cody," she said, feeling awkward and striving for a light tone when Miguel silently shifted away from her, "behave or there's no hamburger with your dinner tonight." The admonishment proved to be unnecessary. His leap out of the tub and the ensuing chase had clearly depleted the last of his energy. Now he sat with bowed head, his expression one of humiliation as he quietly submitted to their ministrations.

Miguel turned toward her. He didn't smile. "I'm sorry," he said softly. "With everything else on your mind, you don't need me mauling you."

"I don't think 'mauling' is quite the word I'd use." Her tone was teasing, but when she saw the genuine regret in his dark eyes, she sobered. "I could have stopped you at any point, Miguel. And I didn't. If you feel you owe me an apology, then I owe you one, too."

He studied her a moment, then nodded silently and returned his attention to Cody.

NIGHT CLOAKED THE WINDOWS by the time they returned upstairs. Miguel busied himself closing drapes in the living room. "You're all wet again," he told Dusty. "There's a robe upstairs on the bathroom door and you can bathe, if you'd like. I'll feed Cody and get dinner started. Then I'll hit the shower. Those dirt roads kick up a lot of dust." His shower would be cold.

"Are you sure you don't need some help?" Dusty asked, following him to the kitchen and watching him read the label on the dog food, then use a measuring cup to fill Cody's bowl. "If you have a flashlight, I can pick vegetables."

"I've got some in the refrigerator we can use. Go ahead and clean up." Cody barked impatiently and Miguel set the bowl down, grateful for the excuse to keep his eyes away from Dusty.

Cody plunged his mouth into the bowl before Miguel could straighten, but when Dusty turned to go upstairs, the dog ran after her. Smart, Miguel thought with a grin. He, too, would rather follow Dusty into the shower than eat. Then he stared at the food left in the bowl and remembered how pitifully thin Cody was. Dusty had fed him tidbits on the drive from the store, but the dog couldn't have had enough to eat in ten minutes. He had to be hungry, yet he'd chosen to leave his food and go with her.

Either Cody had learned his lesson when he'd wandered away from Jack Rose and gotten lost, or he'd never wandered in the first place. Dusty, he knew, wanted to believe the dog had strayed, but she'd admitted that the dog's normal behavior indicated otherwise. Deep in his gut, Miguel knew that something had happened to Jack Rose and Cody had been forced to fend for himself.

He hoped he was wrong. When his father died, he'd had his mother and his sisters for emotional support, but whom did Dusty have? From what little she'd told him, she wasn't close to her mother or her second family.

What about friends? Would she have made close relationships in her Gypsy life-style? If she had, they'd probably be in Moab, where she lived most of the year. When they found her father, dead or alive, would she leave Pinecreek?

He didn't like that idea. Not at all.

DUSTY CAME DOWNSTAIRS with Cody at her heels. The kitchen table was set and the dog bowls were placed against the wall behind a chair. A heavy quilt lay folded in front of the bowls.

"That's your chair," Miguel said, turning from the counter and following her gaze. The dog settled on the blanket and began eating. "Cody seems to want to stay close to you."

"And the quilt?"

"He's still wet and the tile floor is cold."

Dusty smiled. "Some would call you a sucker."

"The vet said he shouldn't get chilled," he said, a touch defensively.

"I call it sweet."

"That sounds better."

They smiled at one another. Dusty raised a hand to the folds of the white terry cloth robe, pulling the lapels to her throat as his gaze wandered over the damp hair she'd left hanging past her shoulders. The look in his eyes was so hot, it seemed to scorch through the bulky fabric and burn her naked flesh.

Her knees felt weak and she sank into her chair. Miguel cleared his throat. "The coals aren't quite ready yet, so I'll take my shower before I put the burgers on." He headed down the hall. "Help yourself to something to drink from the fridge," he called over his shoulder.

Something wet and very, very cold, Dusty decided, rising and opening the refrigerator. The coals might not be hot, but the temperature in the kitchen felt high enough to boil water.

She grabbed a can of beer, but didn't open it at first. She held it to one flushed temple, then to the other. But nothing could cool the flame of desire that every minute spent with Miguel fanned higher.

7

"LET'S MAKE LOVE." Dusty turned from the television screen to face Miguel, who sat at the other end of the couch. Cody lay comfortably ensconced between them, his head in her lap. They'd eaten dinner, cleaned up the kitchen and adjourned to the living room. She rarely watched television, but that wasn't why she had no idea what program was on. She simply couldn't concentrate. Her thoughts alternated between worry over her father and her awareness of Miguel. She couldn't do anything about her father right now, but she most definitely could do something about Miguel.

Miguel seemed to react in slow motion; he moved his gaze from the babbling figures on the screen and faced her. Despite the boldness of her proposition, she discovered that she couldn't quite meet his eyes. She watched his Adam's apple bob up and down as he swallowed. "Are you sure that's what you want?" His voice was husky.

She looked him full in the face, allowing her gaze to rove over his thick hair, the dark eyes fringed with short, thick lashes, the straight nose, the dip above his lips and the tiny cleft in his chin.

"Oh, yes," she assured him, "quite sure."

She'd hoped he'd kiss her, but he didn't move and panic clutched her. Was she wrong? Did he no longer want her?

He stood and extended a hand. "Let's go to bed."

She smiled and slipped her hand into his. Cody stirred and climbed down from the couch to accompany them. "Wait," Miguel said. He hurried to the kitchen, returned with the quilt, then took her hand again and led her upstairs.

He flicked a switch by the bedroom door, and a hurricane lamp on a nightstand cast a soft glow over an antique four-poster bed covered by a blue patchwork quilt. He led Dusty to the bed. She stood still, feeling awkward and beginning to regret her bravado, while Miguel spread the quilt on the floor and showed Cody that he was to sleep there.

She trembled slightly as he straightened and stood before her, reaching out to gently brush her cheek. Eyes downcast, all she could say was, "I'm not really very experienced."

"I didn't think you were," he replied, cupping her chin with one hand. He brushed a light kiss upon her mouth. "You intrigued me from the moment we met. So strong and fearless, yet when I kissed your hand . . . For a moment I saw uncertainty. . . ."

He dropped light kisses across her face, and Dusty let her eyelids flutter closed. His voice fell to a deep murmur. "A vulnerability, as if you weren't quite sure what to do, how to act. A shy little girl peering out of a capable, confident woman. And I kept catching glimpses of her whenever I tried to flirt with you."

Dusty opened her eyes. "I didn't know what to think of you," she admitted. "I decided you were a Restaurant Romeo, out to make it with the new girl."

He pulled back slightly, his face serious. "I've wanted you from the moment we met, but I'm not a promiscuous playboy. I'll take care of precautions, but I'm talking about more than that. I don't make love to just any woman, Dusty. I want you to know that."

"I believe you."

"Good, because I want to feast on you." He held her face with both hands, skimming his thumbs over her eyebrows. "Your eyes are the color of melted milk chocolate," he whispered, "and your hair is the burnished gold of spun taffy." He spread his fingers along her temples, then wove them through her hair, grazing her scalp before following the long strands past her shoulders.

His touch sent tingles slithering down Dusty's spine and she found herself quivering, first in reaction, then in anticipation when he curled his fingers into the robe's lapels. "And your skin. Your tan is the color of caramel." The robe dropped to the floor and his fingertips followed its path down her arms to entwine themselves with hers.

"But your breasts are as white as freshly whipped cream."

Dusty felt her nipples tighten into points. Slipping her hands free, she unbuttoned his flannel shirt and slid it off his shoulders, then unsnapped the fly of his jeans and edged them down.

His low-cut briefs were white against his skin, and the bulge within them bore mute testimony to his desire.

But it was his chest she chose to stroke first. Bare of hair, each sculpted muscle was outlined clearly beneath his satiny-smooth flesh.

She'd been too involved with her own pleasure to dwell on his body before, but did so now. As if sensing her need to explore, Miguel stood passively while she ran her fingertips down the cords of his neck and across his collarbone, then traced the line that divided his chest and curved beneath each pectoral muscle.

She circled those muscles, then rubbed the hard pebbles of his nipples. He sucked in his breath and tightened his stomach, drawing her attention to its flat expanse.

When her hands slid downward, he gripped her waist and claimed her lips, grinding his hips against her, then pushing her back to fall onto the bed. She fell willingly, the sudden, passionate onslaught sapping the strength from her legs. Hands splayed on each side of her, elbows locked, he caught himself rather than land atop her.

He grinned, kissed the tip of her nose, then drew back and slipped his fingers beneath the elastic of her panties. "We match," he murmured at the sight of the plain white cotton, its flat smoothness in counterpoint to his maleness.

"More taffy," he breathed, drawing the cotton down her legs and turning his attention to the golden-brown curls between her thighs. He planted a kiss there, then stood to slip out of his briefs and join her on the bed.

It was a huge bed and they rolled from side to side, bodies rubbing, hands roving, mouths tasting, their senses heating and slickening their bodies with moisture. Dusty moaned as pressure built within her, a surging tidal wave of sensation urged her to meld with Miguel.

He rolled to the side of the bed and reached for the nightstand, his hand fumbling inside the drawer. She covered his smooth back with kisses, flicking her tongue against the moist flesh and savoring its saltiness. She felt rather than heard the groan rise in his chest, then he rolled back and pinned her against the mattress.

Nudging her legs apart with one knee, he knelt between them and bent over her, nibbling a path down to her breasts and suckling at each stiffened nipple before ending his trail in her triangular nest of curls. Trembling and writhing, Dusty shuddered with pleasure, breathing in short, fast gasps as she begged incoherently for him to fill her throbbing emptiness.

Although she couldn't find the words, he understood and sat back on his heels, hands tearing open the wrapper he'd pulled from the drawer. Dusty watched, then sat up and pushed his hands aside to slide the sheath over him herself, then lay back, pulling him with her.

He entered her with a delightful, yet agonizing slowness. She kneaded the muscles of his back as he filled her inch by inch, fusing them into one being. Then he initiated an escalating rhythm that sent their senses spiraling, swelling the tidal waves of sensation higher and higher. Dusty crested first, crying Miguel's name, then felt him pulse deep within her, adding to the ripples of pleasure that still eddied in the depths of her being.

Murmuring in Spanish, he dropped his head beside hers and rolled to one side without withdrawing. They lay quietly while their breathing slowed.

Her head nestled on his shoulder, Dusty felt the rise of a new and unfamiliar joy. Laughter bubbled up within her, bewildering her. She felt strangely, unbelievably happy, yet didn't think it appropriate to laugh after making love. "I vant to drink your blood," she said in her best vampire fashion and nipped his neck with her teeth, making a joke to vent the intoxication she felt.

Miguel threw back his head and exposed his neck. "Lady," he said, chuckling, "you can have anything you want from me."

About to pounce on him, Dusty felt him slip from inside of her and sighed in disappointment.

"Don't go away," he said, kissing the tip of her nose. "I'll be right back." He slid from the bed and into the bathroom, then hurried back. "Now, where were we?" he said, joining her under the covers, where she'd moved, feeling the chill of the room as her flesh cooled.

"You were at my mercy," Dusty said promptly, snuggling into his arms.

"Ah, yes," he agreed, sighing in satisfaction. His familiar grin answered hers as he brushed her hair from her face. "I like a woman who can laugh in bed."

Dusty felt an uncharacteristic giggle rise in her throat. "I can't help it," she admitted. "But I was afraid you'd be insulted if I laughed."

"Why should I be insulted? Lovemaking should make you happy."

"I can't say I've ever felt this happy before." Dusty pretended to ponder his point. "But since you're the expert, you must be right."

"Expert, eh?" Miguel puffed out his chest.

"But then, of course, I don't have much experience to base my opinion on."

Miguel cocked an eyebrow. "I'm sure your instincts led you to the correct conclusion."

"And then again, it could've been a fluke."

"You could be right," Miguel agreed and she blinked in surprise. "Maybe we should try it again to find out."

"Purely for the sake of comparison, of course." Dusty kept her expression deadpan and Miguel nodded, equally serious. She wrapped her arms around his neck. "I guess I'm willing to suffer in the interests of scientific experiment."

She covered his grin with her kiss and sometime later, much later, they declared the experiment a success.

DUSTY WOKE BEFORE DAWN. Slipping from Miguel's side, she rose and showered. Her body felt different this morning, and she washed herself gingerly. Places were tender that had never been tender before. She smiled, remembering the night, then cast the memory aside. Today belonged to her father and her search for him.

Cody greeted her when she came out of the bathroom, but Miguel still slept. Wanting to get moving, she flicked on the bedside light and studied him in a mixture of admiration and irritation, willing him to wake up. His hair was dark against the snowy-white pillow and one dusky-brown arm stretched across her side of the bed. Cody placed his front paws on the bed and nuzzled him. Miguel groaned unintelligibly and rolled away, pulling the sheets over his head. Cody barked.

"What the . . . ?" Miguel sat bolt upright. His sleep-drugged gaze took in Dusty, who stood at the foot of the bed, then swiveled to Cody and back.

"You could have come up with a nicer way of waking me up," he complained. He lay back and petted Cody, who licked his cheek in a good-morning greeting. "I was talking to your mistress," Miguel told him.

Dusty smiled but shook her head, not trusting herself to resist his seduction if he touched her. "Time to go."

"Go where?" He glanced at the dark window. "The sun's not even up!"

"Sergeant Kelly said they'd start the search at dawn. I don't want to miss them, and I have to go home and change."

A guarded expression replaced Miguel's normally forthright one. "I think we can count on them to do their job without us looking over their shoulders."

"Does that mean you don't want to go?" She kept her voice expressionless, but her high spirits wilted. Had she been right about him in the beginning? Now that he'd bedded her, did he want to wash his hands of her?

"That's not what I said." He pushed himself higher and leaned against the headboard. The sheet slipped down and exposed his sculpted chest. She'd caressed every line and curve during the night, she remembered clearly, but the memory only added to her rising sense of betrayal. She crossed her arms beneath her breasts.

"Sergeant Kelly has this number as well as yours," he pointed out, "and he'll call the moment they find anything. I know it's hard to sit and wait, but it's the best thing we can do. We're amateurs and would just get in their way."

"Speak for yourself." She let her tone reflect her icy reaction to what she considered his suggestion that she spend the day in bed with him rather than search for her father. "Not only do I have emergency medical training, I probably know more about wilderness survival than the sergeant or the volunteers. Go back to sleep. I'm sorry I bothered you." She headed for the door.

"Wait! Let's make some coffee and talk about this." He dashed from the bed and caught her by the arm.

She tried to shrug off his hand, but he tightened his grip. "What's there to talk about?" she snapped. "You don't want to go and I don't blame you. Bouncing over bumpy roads isn't everyone's idea of fun. I appreciated your help yesterday, but I don't expect anything else from you." That was a lie and she knew it. Not only had she assumed he'd take her out to join the search today, she'd counted on it.

"I'm not saying that I don't want to go," he retorted. "Let me get dressed and explain over coffee."

Dusty waited impatiently for him to slip into his flannel shirt and jeans, then followed him downstairs and sat at the kitchen table, seething silently while he brewed coffee. In her opinion they were wasting precious time. "Would you at least give me a lift to my apartment so I can get some clean clothes?" she asked when he set a cup in front of her.

"Of course." He sat down across the table and she shifted her gaze away from him. His unbuttoned shirt reminded her of their previous intimacy... and the foolishness of her decision to trust him. "But I don't think you should join the search."

About to sip her coffee, she froze and stared at him over the rim of the cup, then slowly set it down.

"I thought about this last night," he continued. "I understand how much you want to find your father, but you don't know what condition he could be in. Wouldn't you rather remember him as he was when you last saw him, rather than as what the rescue people may find?"

"He's alive!" Dusty slammed her fist onto the table so hard that their cups rattled and coffee sloshed over the rims. She couldn't, wouldn't believe otherwise. "Don't bother making fancy excuses. You don't have to go. I can hitch a ride." She stood, but he rose, too, and grabbed her by the shoulders, forcing her to sit down again. She glared at him.

"I know what it's like to lose a father," he said. "Mine went through the windshield, but Mamá insisted on identifying him. She had nightmares about it for years. Can't you see that I'm trying to protect you?"

"I don't want your protection!" Dusty yelled. "If my father's dead, I want to know how he died. I'm not a weak, pampered female who needs to be treated like some kind of delicate, hothouse flower! And going to bed with me doesn't give you the right to tell me what to do!"

As her anger rose, Miguel's dissipated; now he chuckled. "No, you're a roadside blossom, pretty on the outside but tough as a weed and prickly as hell."

"What's that supposed to mean?" Dusty snapped, suspicious of his change of mood.

He drew her to her feet and into his arms. "No, don't pull away," he whispered, when she splayed her fingers on his chest and kept him at arm's length. "That means you win. We'll go help the search, but you are not to go anywhere without me by your side. Understood?"

"Why?" Stunned by his abrupt reversal, she gaped at him.

"Because I want to be there for you if you get bad news."

"Oh." Not knowing what to say, Dusty stared at him and he kissed the tip of her nose.

"Give me five minutes for a shower, then we'll go by your apartment so you can change, then head straight out. Is that all right?"

"Fine," she answered, still slightly bewildered. She'd won the argument, but somehow felt as if she'd lost the war.

HINTS OF ROSE AND GOLD glimmered on the eastern horizon by the time Miguel drove through Horseshoe Bend and turned onto Forest Service Road 163, but he still had to use the high beams of the truck's headlights to slice through the gloom. Dusty's tension was almost palpable; she leaned forward, straining at the shoulder harness of her seat belt as if she could make him speed up by sheer force of will. But he drove cautiously, feeling his way in a forest made unfamiliar, even foreboding, by the gray shroud of predawn that pressed at the windows of the small cab.

Her expression, dimly illuminated by the dashboard lights, was set and determined. Gone was the easy camaraderie of the previous day, as was the loving rapport they'd shared in bed.

He missed both.

They'd spoken little since stopping at her apartment, where she'd changed into jeans, sweatshirt and sturdy hiking boots. She was intent on finding her father, but he couldn't understand why that meant she had to withdraw from him.

For comfort she'd turned to Cody rather than to him. Miguel had thought Cody would have been better off at home in his yard, but she'd insisted on bringing him and he'd given in—again. Unlike other women he'd dated, he mused with more than a trace of irritation, Dusty made little effort to please him.

The dog lay on the seat between them, his head in her lap. She stared straight ahead, but stroked him constantly. When Miguel reached over to capture her hand, she slipped hers free and resumed her contact with the dog.

He didn't want to believe the rebuff was intentional, but felt it keenly. It sparked an unpleasant thought. Was she using him? She'd accused him of offering to help her search in order to get her into his bed. He could flip the coin and think she'd made love with him as a form of payment.

He didn't like that idea. Not a bit. But how well did he know her? That was the problem with rushing into intimacy, but the magnetism between them had been so strong . . . at least on his side.

Was her silence indicative of regret? He didn't like that idea, either. He simply didn't know her well enough to judge how her mind worked. They were virtual strangers. But that, he swore, would change.

"Penny for your thoughts," he said, then winced when she jerked in surprise. His voice sounded strange, even to his own ears, shattering the gray hush around them.

The expression on her face told him she thought the answer obvious. "I'm thinking of my father out there, alone, maybe hurt . . . and worrying about Cody, I'm sure." Her voice quavered, then steadied, but he heard the effort it took. "How long has it been? How long can he last?"

Not long, Miguel thought. "He has his bedroll and backpack," he said, reminding her of the two things that had seemed to give her hope; he reached for her hand again.

This time she squeezed it. "Yes," she said and lapsed again into silence.

Miguel didn't press her. Her response told him that the gloomy morning had intensified her concern, which was natural. His other worries had been groundless—and unlike him. Dusty was no longer simply an attractive woman who intrigued him. She was a woman he wanted to care for, to protect. He *wanted* her to lean on him, to need him as well as desire him.

That, too, was unlike him.

8

Miguel and Dusty neared her father's camp. When the truck's high beams first picked up the red of taillights, then illuminated horse trailers parked along the side of the road Dusty leaned farther forward, straining at the seat belt harness. She sat back and flexed her shoulders, trying to ease the tension that hunched them.

She'd thought the ride would never end. The assurances she'd given herself that her father could survive, alone in the wilderness, had begun to sound increasingly hollow as they'd driven through the cold, ghostly murk. Eager for action to relieve the dread that was gripping her, she flung open the truck door as soon as Miguel parked. Giving Cody a quick command to stay, she jumped out.

The headlights of several vehicles shone on an open pickup with its tailgate down and two large, stainless steel urns in the back. People bearing foam cups and eating doughnuts milled around it. She headed straight toward them.

Sergeant Kelly was bent over a map spread over the hood of the truck while he conferred with a tall, lean man he introduced as Tom Powell, a deputy with the Forest Service. "We've got four search and rescue organizations out," the sergeant said, offering her coffee and sweet rolls. She refused, but Miguel accepted both.

"With ten to twelve people in each," Sergeant Kelly continued. "They're volunteer groups, but well trained and familiar with the terrain. Since the truck was open and the camp still set up, we'll concentrate in the immediate area today and work outward."

He led them back to the map. "Tom and I worked up a grid around the camp—" his blunt fingertip traced penciled lines "—which we'll check on foot or horseback. Hikers in the shrubby or rocky areas, ten feet apart. Riders in the more open areas, about thirty feet apart."

"Won't that take a lot of time?" Dusty protested. "If he has his bedroll and backpack, he's probably farther away."

"But we don't know for sure if he has them or if they were stolen," the officer reminded her as he folded the map. "When the evidence technicians go over the truck and categorize the contents, we'll have a better idea what the situation is."

Dusty stepped back, involuntarily recoiling as his words undermined her strongest hope for her father's survival. Nighttime temperatures in the mountains could drop below freezing in late September. Images of him depending on pine needles and fallen leaves for warmth made her shudder.

"You'd be surprised," Sergeant Kelly continued "at the number of people that get lost or hurt in the immediate vicinity of their camp."

Not my father, Dusty wanted to insist, but couldn't speak.

The sergeant kept talking. "These searches are slow, but they're methodical. They have to be. We check every nook and cranny a man can squeeze into."

"Fire," she said at last, forcing her voice to work. "He'd light a fire to keep warm—a signal fire if he needed help."

Tom Powell spoke up. "None have been reported in the last month. Of course, a camp fire wouldn't attract attention, and if he's lost but doesn't feel in danger, he might not set a signal fire. He is experienced in back-country camping?" Dusty nodded emphatically. "There are a lot of small streams through these mountains and, with water, he can survive." He smiled encouragement. "If he's here, we'll find him."

Alive or dead? Dusty wondered as she studied the deputy. Judging from the lines in his face and his graying hair, she guessed him to be older than her father, and his eyes were blue rather than brown, but something about him reminded her of Jack—an indefinable air of rugged strength.

Dusty nodded, deciding that she respected this man's opinion and could allow his reassurance to bolster her own confidence. "What can I do to help?"

"We," Miguel corrected, stepping forward.

Sergeant Kelly shook his head. "Best for you to sit tight and let our experienced volunteers take care of this." He eyed Dusty, then added bluntly, "We don't need anybody else missing."

"I can hike fifteen to twenty miles a day with a ninety-pound pack on my back," she shot back, "and I'm also a certified emergency medical technician. I'm no novice."

"You're emotionally involved in this," the sergeant argued. "You've already noticed that this is a slow operation, which is a common complaint of families with missing loved ones. You could rush and overlook something. Trust us to do our jobs, please."

"I can't just sit here!" Dusty turned to the Forest Service deputy, whose expression was more sympathetic.

"We can always use more people on foot," he said. "Did you bring water?"

"We've got juice and soda in the truck," Miguel answered.

Dusty flushed with embarrassment. For hiking they needed the plastic bottles she had in her apartment, bottles that they could hook onto their belts. She'd been in such a hurry to get here that she hadn't thought to bring them.

"I'm sure someone has extra water bottles," Tom said, taking pity on her; Dusty shot him a glance of pure gratitude. "I'll be coordinating in the field and you two can stay close to me."

Sergeant Kelly opened his mouth to object, but Tom cut him off. "I'll take responsibility. They look in good shape to me and I can see they keep to my pace." He turned back to Dusty and Miguel. "I'll call frequent rests, but don't push yourselves." He eyed them both, his face stern until they nodded in unison. "If you need to stop, let me know."

He turned away and called, "Okay, let's get this show on the road." Everyone gathered at the back of the truck, where Tom deferred to the policeman, who, Dusty realized, was coordinating the search from the base camp. He checked the leaders' radios, then told the horseback riders to search through the tall grass as they headed out of the canyon before following the trail around it that led to the higher country.

The sun cleared the horizon and bathed the canyon with light as the riders mounted, the creaking of leather and jangling of tack and spur audible in the quiet dawn. Forming a straight row across the canyon, they started forward at a slow pace, the horses' tails swishing from side to side, their breath steaming in the chilly air. Dusty swallowed hard noticing how high up the horses' legs the grass brushed. At first glance, the canyon appeared unoccupied save for the searchers, but a man in a prone position—a dead man—could easily lie hidden in that tall grass. She swallowed again, then forced her attention back to Sergeant Kelly, who was issuing directions to the hikers.

He assigned Miguel and her to a group that was to search through the rocks, shrubs and trees at the base of the western side of the canyon. Another group would look through the vegetation growing along the stream in the middle of the meadow.

Dusty decided to leave Cody in the truck. She made sure it was parked in the shade, the windows partially opened to give him air. His water bowl was still full and Sergeant Kelly promised to keep an eye on him. Only then did she join Miguel and the other volunteers at the base of the canyon wall.

As they fanned out and wove in and out of the trees, she realized again how much the search centered on looking for a body rather than a living person. She shot a glance to the end of the line where one of the searchers had bent to peer beneath a ledge and her heart contracted painfully; her senses sharpened, waiting for a shout that he'd found a body. But the man straightened and resumed his slow, steady pace.

Suddenly aware that her own steps had lagged, she hurried forward, her glance sweeping the ground beneath trees and shrubs, then checking to her left to see that she kept abreast of the Forest Service deputy. Farther along on his other side, she could see Miguel. The sun shot between the treetops and glinted on his dark hair as he walked, head bent, studying the ground before and on each side of him.

Following his example, she returned her attention to the search. But it wouldn't stay there. She found herself repeatedly looking up and glancing from side to side as the dread within her grew. She could feel tension hunching her shoulders again and swung her arms to try and ease it. She'd never last the morning, much less the day if she remained this keyed up. And she'd go stark, raving mad if Sergeant Kelly forced her to sit and do nothing.

Watch the ground and think of something else, something pleasant, she ordered herself. *Think of Miguel.* A smile curved her lips as she remembered their night of loving. Then she recalled his protective attitude and attempt to tell her what to do. She wouldn't, she swore, put up with the likes of that from any man, no matter how good a lover he was.

She wished they were in Canyonlands where he'd see her in her natural element, backpacking in the wilderness, scaling cliffs, guiding jeeps over dangerous slickrock and rafts through rapids. In control of her own and others' lives. Here in Pinecreek he saw her as a daughter worried about her father—a helpless female, in need of a man's comfort and protection.

The thought made her scowl. She was worried, but she sure as hell wasn't helpless. Hadn't she found Hank on her own? Hadn't she led them to her father's camp?

But, despite what she considered Miguel's attempt to dominate her, she couldn't summon a trace of regret about the way they'd spent the previous night. She'd certainly enjoyed her first experience of passion. Not that she was going to let it—or Miguel—rule her life.

She was a free spirit like her father. Miguel was like her mother, content with home and hearth. She wouldn't repeat her parents' mistake.

Tom called a rest stop when they reached the end of the canyon. Dusty wasn't remotely tired, but sat down obediently. Most of the volunteers were older people, retirees, who probably needed the rest.

"I never thought warm water could taste so good," Miguel said as he joined her and drained his water bottle. The sun, now high in the sky, radiated heat as well as light.

"Tired already?" Dusty teased. He'd removed his flannel shirt and tied it around his waist. His T-shirt, damp with sweat, clung to his muscular chest and she admired him shamelessly.

He shook his head. "Hot, though. I've been going through this water like it was the nectar of the gods."

"Don't worry about running out of water. I'm sure there's more coming." She pointed to a truck that was crossing the meadow toward them. The sun sparkled on the stainless steel of the urn in the open back. When the truck reached them, they found it also contained coolers full of iced sodas.

Miguel emptied a can of soda in what seemed like seconds, then poured water over his head before refilling his water bottle. "I should have thought to bring hats," Dusty said regretfully when one of the other volunteers offered them bandannas to cover their heads.

"You'll know next time," the woman said kindly and moved away to fill her canteen.

"Are you very uncomfortable?" Dusty asked Miguel, thinking she did know better, but as Sergeant Kelly had pointed out, she was too emotionally involved in the search to think rationally. "I'm sure I could get a ride into town if you'd like to go."

His face darkened. "I'm not leaving you alone out here."

"I'm hardly alone," she pointed out, waving a hand in the direction of the people grouped around the water wagon.

"Do I mean as little to you as a total stranger?"

Dusty saw anger flare in his dark eyes and muscles ripple in his cheeks when he clenched his jaw.

"That's not what I mean," she said, picking her words carefully. "This isn't the most pleasant way to spend your day off. I don't want you to feel that you have to stay—"

"I'm here because I want to be," he interrupted. "You don't have to feel dependent on me. *That*'s what you're really afraid of."

He spun away and she stared after him, wanting to call him back but not knowing what to say. Tom shouted the command for everyone to resume their places and she lost the chance.

Confused by her feelings, Dusty joined the line. It went against her grain to depend on anyone. Self-sufficiency was a trait she admired. Miguel had already done so much for her, and all she'd tried to do was give him the option to go about his business.

Unable to come up with any pleasant thoughts to distract herself, she tensed, again anticipating a shout bearing bad news. By the time they reached camp and broke for lunch, her shoulders ached.

Miguel, she saw, headed straight to the food wagon where Sergeant Kelly distributed sandwiches and sodas. Her father's truck was gone, probably taken to the sheriff's office. Feeling neither hungry nor sociable, she let Cody out of the truck and took him with her to sit beneath the shade of a cottonwood tree, where she slumped against its trunk.

"Eat." Miguel stood above her, a sandwich in his hand. She took it rather than argue and he sat down beside her. He also carried sodas and a sandwich for himself. "Kelly called the horse riders in," he said, ignoring Cody's begging. "They haven't found anything, either."

Dusty sat up straighter. "Did he say where the hikers are going next?"

"They're going to ferry us up the trail around the canyon and we're walking down the other side. The vegetation is too thick for the horses. It'll be slow going for us, but at least we'll have more shade."

"Dad would use the trail," she snapped, preparing to go tell the sergeant that.

"Unless Cody ran off and he followed him. You don't know what happened, Dusty. I think Kelly's doing the right thing by combing the entire area. Let him do his job."

Dusty settled back again. Miguel had a point, she conceded reluctantly; besides, if she pushed Kelly too hard, he might take her off the search. "What about the horses? Where are they going?"

"They're following the stream above the canyon."

More content with that course of action, Dusty bit into her sandwich. "Dad might've gone that way looking for gold," she conceded. "Wish I had a horse. I'd rather be with them."

"He could be anywhere. We have as much of a chance of finding him as they do."

Dusty nodded rather than argue. The turkey sandwich tasted like sawdust, so she fed a good quarter of it to Cody.

"He's got his dog food in the truck," Miguel scolded her. "You need that more than he does." She scowled at him and he grinned. "For someone so stuck on independence, you're not taking very good care of yourself. You barely ate last night and didn't even have a doughnut this morning. If you're not careful, I'll think you need a keeper."

Dusty stuffed another quarter of the sandwich into her mouth. "Is that why you're staying?" she asked, after carefully chewing and swallowing the huge bite. "To look after me?"

His grin faded as he studied her. "I don't think you should go through this alone. No matter how tough you are. But if you want me to leave, I will."

Unable to meet his gaze, Dusty stared at the sunlight dancing on a small pool of water at the base of the cliff. She didn't know what Miguel wanted of her or she of him. But she didn't want him to leave. It was nice to look down the line of strangers and see his familiar face and strong, muscular body.

"I like having you here," she admitted, turning to look at him with troubled eyes. "But . . ."

He pressed a finger against her lips. "No buts. That's all I want to hear."

She opened her mouth to speak, but he covered it with his. It was a kiss of such sweet gentleness that all she could do was enjoy it.

When he raised his head, he smiled into her eyes and stroked her cheek with one hand. "Just accept my being here, Dusty Rose. Don't question it." He slid one arm around her shoulders and pulled her against his chest. "Rest. It's going to be a long afternoon."

And it was. Without a trail to follow, the forest was nearly impenetrable. Like Miguel, Dusty had stripped down to her T-shirt during the morning of walking in and out of the hot sun. But fighting her way through and around cat-claw brambles, she needed the long sleeves of her sweatshirt to protect her skin. Despite their frequent rest stops, she was bone tired by the time they reached the canyon floor and her respect for the older volunteers heightened.

When they reached the base camp, dusk had crept among the trees, deepening their shadows. Dusty rushed forward, seeing the riders loading their horses into their trailers. "Did you find him?" she asked eagerly, but the volunteers shook their heads sadly, then averted their eyes and continued coaxing the horses into the trailers.

Stricken, Dusty stood in the middle of the commotion and stared at them. Her emotions screamed for her to beg them not to stop, to keep on searching, but common sense told her that they couldn't search in the dark. Miguel reached her side and slid an arm around her waist, but she stood rigid, refusing to give in to the weakness of comfort.

Tom Powell came up on her other side. "I'm sending some jeeps out," he said gently. "They'll patrol the high trails through the night and we'll be back at dawn to widen the search." The two men led her toward Miguel's truck.

Dusty moved with them automatically. *Another night.* Another long, cold night her father would have to spend alone, maybe hurt, maybe without a bedroll or sleeping bag to keep him warm.

"What about Dad's truck?" she asked, a ray of hope breaking through the fog that enveloped her. "Has Sergeant Kelly heard anything?"

Changing direction, they found him by the water wagon, thanking the hikers and asking them to return the next morning. Dusty spoke up, too, winning grateful smiles from them.

"There are no signs that the truck was broken into," the sergeant told her after the group had dispersed. "But the locks on the cabinets were smashed and someone went through his belongings pretty thoroughly. You don't think he would've left the camper open?"

"Not if he was going to be gone long." Dusty sighed. Nothing made sense.

"Would you like to go down to headquarters tonight and see if there's anything else missing?" the police officer asked. "Or would tomorrow be better?"

"Now," Dusty answered. Maybe she could find something that would give her a clue to what was odd behavior, even for her eccentric father.

9

DUSTY STUMBLED down the concrete steps outside the police station. She would have fallen if it hadn't been for Miguel's supporting arm. The sight of her father's possessions dusted for fingerprints, tagged, bagged and laid out on a long table beneath cold, fluorescent lighting had undone her.

When she'd walked into the room, a flush had heated her flesh; then a chill gripped her and a black haze obscured her sight. The next thing she'd known was the sharp scent of ammonia under her nose and she was seated on a chair, Miguel and Sergeant Kelly hovering over her.

She'd fainted. She still couldn't believe it. But she'd rallied, sat down at that table, and studied every item on it. She read the letter she'd sent to confirm that she'd cleared her schedule for the first week of September...and noticed that the angry one she'd written when her father hadn't shown up in Moab was not there.

It was with the mail the police had obtained from his post office box—mail he'd never picked up. He'd already disappeared.

She'd almost lost control when guilt overtook her—why hadn't she reported him missing, the day he'd failed to arrive in Moab? Miguel had grabbed the smelling salts again, but she'd pushed his hand away and continued to examine her father's belongings. In addition to his bedroll and backpack, his handgun and hunting rifle were missing. So were his compass, binoculars, favorite clothes and personal journals.

A keen observer of nature, Jack took copious notes, she knew, often sharing his findings with both government and private environmental agencies. Whenever he had access to a typewriter, he wrote articles and sold them to magazines and had talked about writing a book. But the journals were of little use to anyone else. He'd developed his own personal shorthand over the years and only he could decipher the chicken scratches he made.

She'd wanted to believe that their absence meant he had them and was further proof that he was safely camped somewhere in the mountains. But the same questions continued to haunt her. Why wasn't Cody with him? Why didn't he pack up his camp and lock his truck? Why didn't he write to cancel their plans?

Sergeant Kelly was equally puzzled. Why would a thief risk taking something so identifiable and apparently worthless? Unless, he'd mused aloud, notes in those journals were valuable, in which case Jack could have been taken to decipher them.

Gold, the officer explained, was an unlikely motive. Mining corporations had sent teams to the Pinecreek area and determined that new microblasting or cyanide leaching techniques were necessary for truly profitable mining, and the local environmentalists were already battling such efforts.

Dusty told him that Jack always detailed the Indian artifacts he'd discovered—and these artifacts would be a bonanza for unscrupulous pothunters. But who in Arizona would've known about them?

Every new lead raised more questions, and Dusty's inability to answer had sapped both her physical and emotional strength. Sergeant Kelly, tired too, had agreed to call it a day.

She let Miguel help her into the truck, then collapsed against the seat, sighing with relief and closing her eyes. Cody nuzzled her hand and slipped his head beneath it, but she had no energy left to pet him.

Climbing behind the wheel and turning on the ignition, Miguel didn't ask her where she wanted to go. If he had, she couldn't have answered. He put the truck into gear and drove off.

"A hot bath and a bowl of my tortilla soup and you'll feel better," he said, braking to a stop and climbing out. Her eyes fluttered open at the sound of his voice, but she stared at him without comprehension before realizing they were at his house. Cody scrambled over her and instinct pulled at her body to follow, but she moved sluggishly, her limbs weighted with lethargy.

Miguel reached in and slid one arm beneath her legs and the other around her back to lift her out. A protest formed in her mind, but emerged as little more than a sigh; she dropped her head to his shoulder when he set her upon her feet. For a moment they stood motionless, then Dusty stepped back and concentrated on putting one foot in front of the other. Cody darted around the yard, then joined them at the door. Yawning, Dusty leaned against a porch post.

When Miguel opened the door, she pushed her body forward and staggered to the kitchen, afraid that if she didn't put food out for Cody immediately, she'd forget. The dog's nails clicked on the tile floor as he followed her.

"I'll do that," Miguel said, taking the bag of dog food from her and filling the bowl. He set it upon the floor, then turned to where she leaned against a counter. "You're exhausted," he said, pulling her close. Dusty burrowed her face in his neck and let him guide her up the stairs to his bedroom. Once there, she tore off her shoes and collapsed in a heap upon the bed.

Miguel turned on the bedside lamp and stared at her. Her face, pale and drawn when they'd left the police station, slowly relaxed as sleep claimed her. Crossing into the bathroom, he got a blanket out of the linen closet and covered her. Very lightly he brushed a stray lock of hair from her face, then bent to kiss her cheek.

She kept too much inside, he mused, returning to the kitchen to start the soup. He'd felt her tension grow throughout the day, had seen her haunted gaze swing from one searcher to the next and guessed that she'd dreaded the discovery of her father's body. But rather than share her fear with him, she'd offered to find a ride back to town and let him leave.

He cursed softly and cut into a carrot with so much force that a piece of it flew across the room. Cody scrambled after it. Why couldn't she lean on him emotionally as well as physically? Crying on his shoulder wouldn't bring her father back, but it might ease the tension and worry hunching those strong shoulders.

Sighing, he dropped the last of the vegetables he'd chopped into a large pot and turned up the flame on the stove until the pot's contents bubbled, then lowered the heat to maintain a simmer.

"Do you think we should wake Dusty?" he asked Cody, who lay at his feet, eyes watching the floor for more tidbits. Apparently he'd adapted to his new environment and no longer needed to keep an eye on her. The dog looked at him, then rose and walked to the blanket by his bowl, where he lay down again and closed his eyes.

"No, eh?" Miguel prompted. Cody reopened one eye, then closed it again. "Well, what do dogs know?" he added, then decided to let her sleep for a few more minutes while he called to check on her Willys. The garage was closed, but since he was a friend of the mechanic as well as a customer he called him at home.

The carburetor was clogged and needed rebuilding. Although salvageable, it wouldn't be ready until the end of the week. Pleased, Miguel smiled. That meant Dusty would continue to need him. He wasn't sure what would happen when she was free to come and go without him. Issuing directions to give the entire engine a thorough examination and bill the cost to him, he cut short the mechanic's glowing praise of the old car. Dusty, he knew, would never sell it, especially if it was all she had left of her father besides memories.

Hanging up, he climbed the stairs to draw her bathwater. He had neither bubble bath nor bath oil, but added mineral salts, which softened the water and soothed aching muscles. Awakened by the sound of the running water, he saw Dusty eye him drowsily when he came out of the bathroom.

"Time for your bath, then dinner," he said, stretching out beside her.

She yawned, mumbled something unintelligible and curled up against him. Her lips pressed a kiss against his neck, then she rested her head upon his shoulder. Miguel held her a moment, fighting his desire. The long day had tired him, too, but if he made love to her now, they might both fall asleep; and Dusty needed to eat to keep her strength up.

"Bath time, madam," he said as though he were a servant. He sat up, but she didn't move. "Shall I undress you?"

Murmuring assent, she lifted her arms over her head and stretched. Needing no further encouragement, he lowered the blanket and gripped the hems of her sweatshirt and T-shirt and worked them up and over her head, exposing her breasts. Reacting to the cool air, her nipples slowly puckered and stiffened. Unable to resist, he lowered his head and drew first one, then the other into the warm recesses of his mouth while his fingers worked the catch on her jeans.

She sighed in pleasure, lowering her arms to stroke his head and run her fingers through his hair. Trailing kisses down her flat stomach, Miguel moved out of reach. If she brought his head to hers and kissed him, he knew he couldn't be able to resist making love to her.

Instead, he pulled off her jeans and walked her to the bathroom. The bright light made her blink, but seeing the full bathtub she stepped out of her underpants.

Like the ones she'd worn the day before, they were a bikini cut, but made of cotton, betraying her practical nature. He wondered if she owned any satin or lace. If he bought her some, would she wear them for him? Not that it made a difference. He could very well grow fond of cotton—even burlap, haircloth or sandpaper—if they were on her body.

Deciding he needed to get out of there now, before he joined her in the inviting waters, he mumbled something about dinner and dashed into the kitchen to give the soup a quick stir.

DUSTY LET HERSELF SINK deeper into the warm water while Miguel was gone. Like all bathtubs the old claw-foot tub was too short for her long legs, but at least it was deep enough to nearly cover her knees when she bent them. She lay quietly, allowing the heat to drain the tension from her muscles.

As her body relaxed, her mind awoke and the guilt she'd repressed at the police station rushed back. She'd wasted a week waiting for her father in Moab, then another finding a room and a job in Pinecreek. Yet another week researching gold mining in the area and exploring the mountainous back roads on her own. She moaned and sat up. Drawing her knees to her chest and wrapping her arms around them, she let her head droop.

She'd failed her father.

No one else kept track of his comings and goings. His friends were always happy to see him, but he moved in and out of their lives without question.

She leaned back and looked up when Miguel returned. He turned off the bright bathroom light and set something upon the vanity by the sink. She heard the clinking of glass and the striking of a match just before a soft glow filled the room.

He moved aside and she saw the tall, delicate glass sphere of an antique oil lamp. "Lovely," she murmured.

"Not as lovely as you," he responded, his gaze sweeping her naked body, then settling on her breasts. "Feeling better?" he asked, coming forward to kneel by the side of the tub. She nodded, but the smile she offered him wavered.

"What's wrong?" he asked quickly.

"I should have contacted the authorities the day Dad didn't show up in Moab," she exclaimed, stricken. "He could be dead by now and it's all my fault!"

"You quit your job and came looking for him," Miguel reminded her. "You didn't just go back to work and forget about him." He pulled her close and pressed her face into his shoulder. "Go ahead and cry," he urged, "let it out."

She didn't want to cry, didn't want pity. She wanted to find her father, wanted to prove her fears groundless.

And right now she wanted Miguel. Wanted his touch to inflame her senses and overwhelm her mind. He stroked her back, murmuring soft words of tender sympathy, but she wanted passion rather than compassion and raised her head to kiss him, cutting off his flow of words.

He kissed her back and she slipped her hands beneath his arms. Taking him by surprise, she pulled his upper body over the edge of the tub and into the water on top of her.

Sputtering, he lifted his mouth from hers, but she spoke first. "If you're going to join me in the bath, Miguel," she said innocently, letting her hand begin an exploratory path down his chest, "I suggest you take your clothes off."

He did.

BY THE TIME they got downstairs, the soup was beginning to smell scorched. Miguel whisked it off the heat and stirred it carefully. He cut corn tortillas into strips, fried them in oil, then ladled the soup into two bowls while Dusty watched. He sprinkled the tortilla chips and grated Monterey Jack cheese over the top, then brought the bowls to the table.

He set a bowl in front of her and she sniffed at the pungent aroma of tomatoes, peppers and spices. "If it tastes half as good as it smells, it's going to be wonderful." She dipped in a spoon and blew lightly to cool the hot liquid before she slipped the spoon into her mouth.

"It is," she said when she'd swallowed. "*When* we find my father, I'll take you out camping and cook you a feast. I seem to be all thumbs in a kitchen, but the outdoors inspires me."

"I'd like that," he said, but fixed his dark eyes on her intently, seeming to ask a question.

"It's a date, then." Dusty smiled, but wondered if they were thinking of the same question. Would they still see each other when the search for her father was over? She'd never planned to stay in Pinecreek.

Ducking her head to break eye contact, she took another mouthful of soup. The thought of never seeing Miguel again set off a curious ache in her chest. But how could she stay in Pinecreek? Waiting tables was simply a means to make as much money as possible in the least amount of time, leaving her free to indulge her love of the outdoors. She couldn't see herself doing it year round.

You could marry him and have his babies, a voice whispered in her head, and she almost choked on the next spoonful of soup. "Went down the wrong pipe," she told Miguel and coughed.

Assuring him she was all right, she lapsed into silence. That had been her mother's voice, she knew, an echo of the innumerable lectures she'd delivered on the proper role of woman. Despite the lectures, Dusty had opted for a very different life-style, and marriage to Miguel definitely didn't fit into that picture.

On the rare occasions she envisioned a future with a man, she imagined one who felt the call of the wilderness, who shared her love of nature. Not a man tied down to the obligations of a business and family.

The kind of marriage she envisioned was like the one between two former tour guides who'd saved their money and opened a four-wheel-drive vehicle rental service in Moab. Both complained about paperwork and days confined to the office, but they divided those chores, as well as their domestic duties equally.

What Miguel needed was a woman like her mother, but Dusty was too much like her father. If either tried to change for the other, they'd make one another miserable. Just like her parents.

She couldn't ask for a better lover or a friend than Miguel, but she wouldn't allow passion to blind her to the impossibility of a future with him.

"I suppose it's too late to call about the Willys," she said, to divert her mind from the thought that while she still didn't feel as if she *needed* Miguel, she'd miss him when she left Pinecreek. A lot.

"I already did." He explained what the mechanic had told him and Dusty sighed with relief. Rebuilding the old carburetor was cheaper than replacing it and wouldn't totally deplete her rainy-day savings.

"How long can you keep Juan's truck?" she asked.

"As long as we need it. More soup?" He picked up his bowl and stood, stretching out his other hand for hers.

"Please." She stared at his broad back as he dished out more soup and marveled at how he'd said we. "What about work tomorrow?" she asked rather than question that we. She hadn't forgotten his flare of temper when she'd suggested she get a ride back to town with one of the searchers, so that Miguel could return home.

"What about it?" he asked, returning to the table.

Dusty's glance slid away from his face. "The search could last until dark again," she pointed out.

"We can leave a little early and still make it to work."

Dusty couldn't believe her ears. Where had the kind, understanding Miguel she'd come to know gone? "You think my waiting tables is more important than looking for my father?"

"It's not like there's no one else searching." When she continued to stare at him incredulously, Miguel passed a hand over his eyes as if to block out the sight. "Don't look at me that way, Dusty." She didn't blink.

He shoved his bowl away and stood abruptly. "I don't like the idea of leaving you alone." He moved around the table to reach for her, but she reared away.

"Listen to me closely, Miguel," she said, standing to face him angrily. "I've been rattling around the back-country of Utah for seven years now. Alone or with people who are dependent on me. Not vice versa. I do not need you or any man's protection!"

"I know, I know!" He threw up his hands in exasperation. "You're a roadside weed, not a hothouse flower!" He glanced upward as if praying for patience, then faced her with calm determination. "But you're also a woman under a great deal of stress. If I leave you to search until dark and you have to go home to that camp you call an apartment, you're going to sit and worry. I can't be with you. I *have* to go to work."

"I'm not stopping you."

"Don't I mean anything to you?"

Standing nearly nose to nose with him, Dusty tried to stare him down. He didn't retreat an inch.

He wanted an answer. How did she feel about him? Did the fact that she'd even considered the thought of marriage mean she loved him? Where did passion cross the line into love?

She didn't know enough about relationships between men and women to even guess. All she knew was that she didn't want to make the mistakes her parents and Wayne had. Regardless of how happy her mother was with Fred, she didn't want a marriage like theirs. She couldn't bear to be a housewife cooped up in a house all day. Outdoors she could sit and watch a bird build a nest for hours, but indoors she grew restless.

If loving Miguel meant tying herself to him and to his home in Pinecreek, then she couldn't—wouldn't—love him. But, her honest nature asked, if her feelings for him weren't love, what were they?

"I don't know," she finally answered, turning away and sinking onto her chair. Propping her elbows on the table, she covered her face with her hands. "I just don't know. There's so much going on and everything's happening so fast between us."

She heard him move around the table and resume his seat. "I can't argue with that," he admitted. She slid her hands down to support her chin and studied him. The straight line of his mouth drooped with disappointment, then he sighed.

"Okay, we'll table that discussion for now. To go back to the subject of working, I want you to consider how emotionally involved you are in the search. The other volunteers go home and resume their lives. With nothing else to occupy your mind, you'll go home and worry. Right?"

Dusty nodded reluctantly.

"If you come in to work," he continued in a flat, neutral tone, "you'll give your mind—and your emotions—a rest, and you'll be that much more refreshed the next day."

"How would I ever concentrate?"

"Habit. You're the only one on the floor until Friday, when Ramona comes in. Once you get busy, you won't have time to think of anything else."

Dusty started slightly and shifted her gaze. She'd forgotten that his youngest sister only worked weekends. She'd come in on school nights because Dusty was training.

Preferring to cook, Carmen hadn't waited tables in years, and Luisa was out of the question. Since Carmen had lost her first child to a miscarriage, Mamá Rosa refused to allow Luisa to carry anything heavier than a menu. If Dusty didn't work, Ramona would have to.

She turned back to Miguel. His face, like his voice, was expressionless. He'd withdrawn from her. Their relationship no longer had anything to do with her decision. He was presenting his argument as though she were a stranger.

She dropped her gaze to the table, where her fingers toyed with the fringe on the place mat. She preferred his anger, she realized. This cold neutrality cast her adrift, gave her nothing to fight against.

She'd rather he bellow and point out everything he'd done for her, and insist that she return the favor by working. But that wasn't his way. He wanted her to work because he thought that would be best for her.

She covered her eyes with one hand to hide the silly tears suddenly gathering in her eyes. Gratitude, she told herself, that was what she was feeling and why she felt an almost overwhelming urge to move around the table, haul him to his feet and hug him so hard his ribs could crack.

He was right, she decided, and the admission dissolved the threat of tears. She was emotionally strung out. If she waited tables and got her mind off her worry, her subconscious could run on automatic and she might remember something important.

"We'll join the search at dawn?" she asked.

"And stay until three. That'll give us an hour and a half to get back, clean up, change and get to the restaurant in time for dinner."

"You and your mother certainly worry about eating a lot," Dusty complained. She'd prefer to use the extra half hour before the restaurant opened for the search.

"Our days will be long," he responded, "and we'll need to keep up our strength." He paused. "Does that mean you'll work?"

She nodded, deciding not to argue about the half hour.

"Thank you." The neutral mask disappeared from his face and his grin took its place.

"No, thank you," she said, smiling, too. When he rose she stood and met him halfway. She'd expected one of his gentle busses, but not a tinge of gratitude colored his kiss. By the time he raised his head, she had to lean against him for support.

"Do you want any more soup?" he asked, his voice husky.

"Just you," she replied and pulled his head down for another of his delicious, long, hot, wet kisses. Without lifting his head, he nudged her gently toward the stairs. They had to end the kiss to mount the steps, but their hands worked busily, leaving a trail of clothes behind them.

Miguel slowed the pace when they fell across his bed. His hands and lips traced her body while he spoke softly in Spanish. Unable to understand the words, Dusty heard their rhythmic cadence like a liquid melody that accompanied their lovemaking. And as the tempo of their movements changed, so did the lilt of his voice.

"¡Yo te quiero!" he cried when they peaked then repeated those words more softly as their bodies grew still and their breathing calmed. He said them again as he covered her face with kisses. Then he raised his head and stared into her eyes with uncharacteristic gravity.

"Yo te amo," he declared formally.

Dusty smiled at him uncertainly, then rested her cheek against his smooth chest.

She wondered what the Spanish phrases meant, but was afraid to ask.

10

THE SEARCH THE NEXT DAY was as fruitless as the previous one. Dusty remained true to her word and left with Miguel for the restaurant. When they arrived at La Margarita, Miguel's family gathered around them. Even Ramona was there.

Mamá Rosa spoke first. "We read about your father in the newspaper. Our family knows what it is like to lose a loving man. We are very, very sorry." She hugged Dusty, then lifted the corner of her apron to dab at her eyes.

"The police are advertising a reward for information," Ramona told her. "I am sure he will be found, but if you don't feel like working, I will."

Dusty couldn't answer as Carmen and Luisa stepped forward to express their sympathies and embrace her. Even the teenagers who served as dishwashers and busboys offered their awkward, yet earnest, condolences.

Touched by their concern, Dusty swallowed heavily. For a woman who hated to cry, she thought, clinging to irony to maintain her composure, she'd been moved to tears repeatedly in the last week.

"Thank you," she managed to say, reaching for Miguel's hand and squeezing it.

"Mi hijo," Mamá Rosa said, her gaze fastening on their linked hands, "he is comforting you?"

"She means me," Miguel explained, "her son."

"Yes," Dusty answered honestly, aware that she'd inadvertently revealed the change in their relationship. "Miguel is being very helpful."

"Good." Mamá Rosa stepped back and smoothed her apron over her hips. "As my oldest, he especially knows what it is like to lose a loving father. A woman needs the heart and arms of a strong man in such a bad time."

"I'm very grateful to him," Dusty mumbled, blushing slightly at the thought of everything she'd been doing in Miguel's arms.

"Now you must eat and tell us all about it," Mamá Rosa said, leading her to the table. "But, as Mona said, you do not have to work if you don't want to."

"I'll work." Dusty turned to Ramona. "I know you need to study and I need to keep busy."

"That is wise, *mi hija,"* Mamá Rosa said. "You arc strong. *Mi hijo* needs such as you."

Mi hija meant my daughter, Dusty learned as Mamá Rosa drew her deeper into the folds of the Santiago family in the following days. As Miguel had predicted, working provided a welcome relief from the strain of searching for her father. But the distraction of work failed to prod any new clues out of her subconscious, despite a second examination of Jack's belongings, and she grew increasingly frustrated. A few people came forward in response to the publicity, but their tips all led back to the camp they'd already found.

Mamá Rosa always bustled forward when they arrived at the restaurant, her sharp eyes reading Dusty's face before she hugged her and led her to the table to eat. Not all of the affection the older woman lavished on her rose from sympathy, Dusty suspected. Much of it stemmed from her approval of the relationship blossoming between Miguel and Dusty.

Dusty couldn't have kept it a secret, if she'd wanted to. Not only did they arrive and leave together, but Miguel never missed an opportunity to touch her. And she could no longer ignore him when he held a door for her or stood until she sat down at the dinner table so he could scoot her chair forward. Such gestures were a part of his courteous, considerate nature, and she learned to accept them with a soft smile.

She also found herself accepting gifts of items she once would have scorned. Scented bubble bath, lotions and cologne from Mamá Rosa, lingerie from Carmen and Luisa. "You need to pamper yourself," they told her, "to keep your spirits up." While she appreciated the thought behind the gifts, it was Miguel who appreciated the satin and lace adorning her body when she came to his bed at night. She teased that she couldn't understand why, since he never left it on her for very long. But she discovered a new level of joy in pleasing him.

The slick glide of satin against her skin... the softness of her sun-dried skin as it had absorbed the soothing, rich creams... the heady scent of musk... the peekaboo lace that revealed more than it hid. With Miguel she entered a whole new realm of sensual experience and for the first time reveled in her body as a source of pleasure.

When Ramona came in to work on Friday, she was quick to notice the change in Dusty. "You seem to be getting along quite well with Miguel," she commented when they were alone at their station.

"You were right about him. He's very nice." To evade Ramona's knowing grin, Dusty reached for a stack of napkins and began to fold them.

"*¿Vas a dar a mi hermano hijos fuertes que puedan llevar el apellido Santiago?*"

Turning back to her, Dusty eyed her friend suspiciously. "You sound so much like your mother I'm almost afraid to ask what you're saying."

"Miguel is the last of our line to carry the name of Santiago. I was wondering if you planned to give him strong sons. It would make Mamá very happy." Ramona smiled, but her expression demanded an answer.

"It's a bit early to be talking marriage," Dusty mumbled, resuming her folding, "much less kids. Don't you think?"

"What about love?"

"A little early for that, too." Dusty kept her gaze on the napkins. "I've only known him a few weeks."

"What about love at first sight?"

"It doesn't last!" Cornered, Dusty shoved the napkins aside and looked up. "And I've seen what that's like firsthand."

"You've been hurt," Ramona guessed.

"My parents," Dusty explained with a sigh, "never should have married and had a baby. I can remember some raging battles and now that I'm older, I think there must have been some raging lovemaking afterward.

That's the only reason why they could've stayed together for as long as they did."

"Besides you," Ramona put in.

Dusty shook her head. "Once I reached school age, I was the excuse for my mother to try and force my dad to live the way she wanted. And when he couldn't, she took me and left him. A child needs security and stability," she said, quoting her mother.

"You don't think that's true?"

Dusty considered. After all the years of resentment and arguements with her mother, she tried for the first time to put herself in her place. Thought about how she would feel if she had a baby.

"I guess I can see her point, but . . ." Her voice failed as she tried to put her feelings into words. "I never felt safer or more secure than when I was with my father. He . . ."

"Loved you," Ramona finished for her as Dusty blinked rapidly. "You don't have to talk about him. I understand."

But she wanted to. "He always had a smile," she whispered past the lump in her throat, "and a story for me. He always put a roof over our heads, clothes on our backs and food on the table. It wasn't as though we lived from hand to mouth."

She felt an arm slip around her waist and discovered Mamá Rosa standing beside her. "You are talking about your father?" she asked. Dusty nodded. "Continue," the older woman said, gently squeezing her waist.

"Sometimes a roof leaked, but he always fixed it. He could fix anything. He just couldn't bear to be confined to an office job, and to my mother that meant he couldn't provide security and stability. He was a good worker, though. The Park Service rehired him every year for the busy season, and he always found other jobs for the winter, even if we did move around a lot."

Dusty didn't know why, but she felt it important for these two women to see her father from her viewpoint rather than her mother's.

"He's honest and responsible. He never missed a child support payment and always paid my airfare to visit him in the summers. His priorities in life just aren't getting ahead and making a lot of money."

"And for this reason your mother divorced him?" Mamá Rosa asked.

"She said his life-style wasn't fit for raising a child."

"She had to do what she thought was right for her and for you," Mamá Rosa said slowly. "As long as he loved you and provided for you, I think she was wrong. But that is easy for me to say. I believe that if you love someone, you love him as he is, not how you want him to be."

"Do you think there is such a thing as love at first sight, Mamá?" Ramona asked.

The older woman shook her head. "How can you love someone without knowing him?"

"What if you know one another and know you want different things in life?" Dusty asked.

Mamá Rosa smiled. "You find a compromise because what you want most in the world is the other. And you never let yourself forget that." She stepped back to glance into the dining room. "Luisa is seating one of Ramona's tables. Time to go to work." She turned away as Ramona left to greet her customers, but Dusty called her back.

"Mamá—" she'd long ago dropped the Rosa "—how do you know that love will last and make the compromise worthwhile?"

The smaller woman looked up with a gentle expression on her face. "You must trust in yourself, and . . ." she paused, her dark eyes studying Dusty slyly, "in the man you love." She patted Dusty's cheek. "Do not worry. *Mi Miguelito* will take good care of you and your babies." She winked and hurried to the kitchen.

But that means all the compromising will be on my side, Dusty protested silently. She was used to taking care of herself, and Miguel had already shown a marked tendency to tell her what to do in his efforts to "protect" her. That trait could only worsen if she married him and had his babies.

Would love make up for the loss of her independence?

Was independence lonely?

She remembered Wayne and the past year of pain he'd felt after Rachel left him. Was that what lay in store for her if she left Miguel and returned to Moab?

She needed answers to her questions. Piece by piece, her clothes were joining Miguel's in his closet. And when they'd picked up her Willys from the garage on the way to work that afternoon, he'd suggested she cancel the lease on her studio apartment.

He'd asked for nothing in return, not even rent money, much less love. He'd pointed out that her landlord probably didn't allow pets and even if he did, Cody wouldn't have the fenced yard that Miguel's house provided.

All good arguments, yet she'd refused to give up her apartment. With somewhere else to go, she didn't feel so dependent on him. Not that she didn't like staying with Miguel. She did. Did that mean she loved him?

Ramona broke into her thoughts. "Luisa sat you. Time to quite daydreaming about Miguel and make some money." More than happy to comply, Dusty rushed to the table.

TO DUSTY'S RELIEF, Miguel did not renew the subject of her moving in with him. The search for Jack Rose dragged on another week. The grid on Sergeant Kelly's map circling her father's camp grew so wide that the sheriff's department authorized the use of a helicopter with a heat-seeking device. Searchers with four-wheel-drive vehicles drove to the occupied areas pinpointed by the pilot. Tom Powell arrested a few people for hunting out of season, but no one found any sign of Jack.

The following Monday, Dusty and Miguel returned to the base camp to find it deserted save for two men who stood by a small fire, warming their hands. Although the deepening dusk made it difficult to discern their features, she recognized the shapes of Sergeant Kelly and Tom Powell. They would, she knew, feel it was their responsibility to remain in camp until every volunteer returned safely.

"Sorry we kept you waiting," she called, climbing out of Willys to join them. The men dropped their hands to their sides and stood stiffly, staring at her in silence as she approached. Her footsteps faltered. Something was wrong. She swung her head from side to side, frantically examining the camp, probing the shadows . . . looking for her father's body.

"Tell me!" Dusty demanded, stopping where she was, unable to move another foot forward until she knew. "Don't beat around the bush!" Miguel caught up with her and his hand on the small of her back guided her the remaining distance to the two men.

"I'm calling off the search," the policeman told them without preamble. "With the helicopter, we've covered hundreds of miles. He either isn't here or . . ."

"He's dead," she finished brutally when he hesitated. "That's what you think, isn't it?" She heard the pitch of her voice rise to a shriek, but didn't care.

"Dusty," Miguel murmured. He slid his arm from her back to her waist, trying to soothe her, but she ignored him.

"You can't know for sure, but you're just going to give up! Just walk away and forget there's a human being out there!" She indicated the mountain rising above them with an angry wave of her arm.

"I'm sorry, Dusty," Sergeant Kelly said, keeping his voice soft. "He's been missing for as long as six weeks. We'll keep the bulletins posted, and both the sheriff's department and the Forest Service will keep an eye out for him, but we can't justify concentrating this many man-hours any longer." He met her furious gaze without flinching. "We've done the best we could."

He turned and walked away, his shoulders slumping with the air of a defeated man, but Dusty didn't relent. She stared after him, with hatred, then looked at Tom

Powell, softening her expression in silent appeal, but he shook his head sadly.

"I wish there were more we could do," he said with a sigh. "But all we can hope for now is that he walks down from those mountains one of these days and makes us look like fools."

"Thank you." Miguel spoke when Dusty remained silent. "Thank you for everything you've done. Tell Sergeant Kelly that, too, would you?"

Tom nodded and reached out to squeeze Miguel's shoulder. Dusty saw him turn toward her, but crossed her arms in a gesture of denial and refused to look at him.

"Take care of her," Tom told Miguel. "She needs you."

MIGUEL WAITED PATIENTLY while Dusty stared into the fire. Waited for her to turn to him. When she didn't, he wrapped both arms around her waist. She shivered and leaned back against him. At least she was accepting his warmth. Slight tremors coursed through her body, betraying her inner turmoil.

"Let's go home," he suggested softly. She started, as if roused from a dream, and lifted her head to gaze into the shadows beyond the circle of light.

"My father's out there," she insisted, "and I'm going to find him!"

"It's too dark now." Because he, too, thought further effort useless, Miguel didn't trust himself to say more. Putting out the fire, he led her to the Willys and ushered her into the passenger seat. When he took her usual place behind the steering wheel, she handed him the keys in silent acquiescence.

Once they got home, she moved like a robot set on remote control. She fed Cody and gave him a perfunctory pat on the head. She offered to help prepare dinner and silently chopped the vegetables Miguel handed her. She ate mechanically, thanked him politely, took her dishes to the dishwasher, then announced she was taking a shower and going to bed.

Hesitating only a moment, Miguel followed her upstairs and hovered outside the bathroom door. Perhaps, he thought, she was seeking solitude to give vent to her pain, like an animal that goes off to die alone. He eased the door open slightly after the water had run for a few minutes, but Dusty made no sound.

Leaning an arm against the doorjamb and resting his forehead on it, he waited. At that moment he hated Jack Rose, hated him for the torment he'd inflicted on his daughter, however unintentional.

The loss of his own father had been painful, but at least it had been a quick, clean cut. A good-bye kiss in the morning with a promise of a present when he returned. A telephone call that afternoon.

But without a body there could be no casket, no service to commemorate the loss of a loved one. No final good-bye, no certainty. Only stunned grief and bewilderment . . . and a swirl of unanswerable questions.

When the shower stopped, he closed the door and backed away. Still no sound from Dusty. She was, he guessed, clinging to her stubborn hope and blind faith in her father's ability to survive in the wilderness.

He cursed softly and sat down on the edge of the bed. Part of him admired her strength, another part wanted to shake her and force her to accept that her father was gone. He was tired of spending his days bouncing over rutted roads and tramping through the forest. If fifty people couldn't locate Jack Rose, how could Dusty think he still lived?

Miguel was anxious for them to begin concentrating on *their* relationship. His feelings had deepened and he needed to know that he was as important to her as she'd become to him. He wanted her to turn to him, to let him hold her while she cried.

Somehow he had to convince her to accept her loss and get on with her own life. With him.

Dressed in an oversize T-shirt, Dusty came out of the bathroom. "Were you waiting? You should have told me. I would've hurried."

"No rush." He studied her, but saw no sign of tears. Her eyes were clear, if dull.

"I'm all right, Miguel," she said with a wan smile. "You don't need to hover over me like a mother hen. I'm disappointed that Sergeant Kelly called off the search, but that doesn't mean I'm giving up."

"Maybe you should." He kept his voice low, but she heard him. Her eyes widened and she sucked in her breath. He rose from the bed and approached her. She didn't retreat, but her stance stiffened, warning him not to touch her. Her chin came up and a spark of anger lighted her eyes.

"You, too?" she asked scornfully. "You think I should just give up?"

Miguel sighed and ran a hand through his hair. He kept his voice reasonable. "What can you do that nearly fifty people and a helicopter couldn't?"

"I'll think of something," she insisted, but her gaze slid to the floor and he knew she had no idea what to do.

"Give it a rest for a few days," he urged. "We can sleep in tomorrow, then take my car down into the desert. The weather is perfect this time of year. We'll take the top down, soak up the sun and let the wind blow through our hair." She still didn't look at him, but she was listening, which encouraged him.

"We can find a secluded spot and picnic, take our clothes off, sunbathe in the nude. It will do you good, Dusty, I know it will."

She raised her head and looked at him with sorrow-shadowed eyes. "I'll think about it," she said quietly. She leaned forward and kissed him gently, then climbed into bed.

Miguel hurried through his shower, but when he returned she was asleep, her breathing deep and even. He climbed in beside her and planted a soft kiss upon her cheek. *Tomorrow*, he told her silently, *the healing will begin*.

MIGUEL WASN'T SURE what woke him, but knew instantly that Dusty was not beside him. He bolted upright when she came out of the bathroom. Slivers of the dawn's early light peeked through the gauzy curtains over the bedroom window and he saw she was fully dressed.

"What are you doing?"

"You're awake," she said, halting at the bedroom door.

"Damn right," he growled, tossing back the covers. "Where the hell are you going?" He stood and marched to the bedroom door, blocking it.

"Back to Dad's camp. There must be something I've missed."

"And you were going to sneak out without telling me?"

"I was going to leave you a note."

"A note!" Miguel felt his hands knot into fists; he turned and slammed one into the door. "Did you stop to consider that I might worry about you out there alone?"

"I can take care of myself. Why should you worry? I thought I'd be nice and let you sleep."

The honest bewilderment in her voice infuriated him all the more. "I'll worry because I love you!" he shouted, swinging back to face her. "And I don't want whatever happened to your father to happen to you. You say he could take care of himself, too, and he's been missing for over a month!"

His outburst had shocked her into silence. It had certainly shocked him. He couldn't discern her features in the dim light, and the only sound in the room was that of his own labored breathing.

"What do you think I've been telling you when we've been making love?" he added, unable to bear the silence. "*¡Yo te quiero, yo te amo!* I want you, I love you! I've never said those words to another woman. I told you in Spanish because I didn't have the guts to say it in English." He paused, praying she'd reach for him, tell him she returned his love. Instead she stood in front of him, immobile.

"I kept hoping you'd ask me, but you never did," he added and waited again, but still she neither spoke nor moved. "Say something, please."

"I..." she began, but her voice trembled and he heard her take a deep breath. "I don't know what to say, Miguel." Moving with uncertain steps, she crossed to the bed and sat down.

"How about 'I love you, too'?" he suggested, joining her on the bed and sliding an arm around her. She raised her face to his, her eyes huge, but not filled with joy as he'd hoped. He saw uncertainty and confusion.

"I'm not sure I know what love between a man and a woman is," she murmured. "I know I care about you, Miguel, I really do." She paused, her eyes begging him to believe her. "But right now, all I can think of is my father. I have to go out there again, and I have to go alone."

Miguel shook his head, not trusting himself to speak. He'd finally found a woman he could love for the rest of his life, but all she could say was that she cared about him. For the first time he could understand how the women who'd sworn their love for him had felt. He'd told them that he'd cared for them, too. The irony made him grimace.

Mona had been right when she'd warned that this time he could be the one hurt. Moving stiffly he withdrew his arm from Dusty, then stood and turned his back upon her.

"I'll be all right," she said. "Please, don't worry about me. I'll take Cody with me."

A strangled laugh escaped the tightness in his throat. "Oh, fine. He did your father a lot of good."

He heard the swift intake of her breath, knew his bitterness had hurt her, but didn't care. The creak of the bed told him she'd risen, but no footsteps moved toward the door.

"Miguel . . ." Her voice was soft, pleading.

He crossed to the window. "Just go," he said harshly, yanking on the drapes to open them. "Do what you have to do."

She went.

11

FROST RIMMED THE TREES as Dusty took the now familiar road leading into the high mountains. The cottonwoods lining the stream into the canyon where they'd found her father's truck had lost their golden autumnal canopy at some point in the past few weeks. She wasn't sure when.

Her breath steamed in the crisp October air when she climbed out of her Willys and walked around the site of the abandoned camp. Cody ambled from spot to spot, nose to the ground, but the scent of the searchers had obliterated any trace of her father.

She walked as aimlessly as the dog, her gaze fixed on the forest above the canyon walls. Miguel was right, she thought, recalling their conversation from the previous night, but blocking out the morning. What could she hope to do alone?

But how could she just walk away and resume her life? Waves of helplessness washed over her, draining her strength, and she sat down on a rock. Pulling her knees to her chest and wrapping her arms around them, she lowered her head.

She missed Miguel. Missed his presence by her side, his calm reassurance, his caring, gentleness and strength. His support. She'd begun to depend on him. Did that mean she loved him?

He'd said he loved her...but she couldn't think about that now. Cody joined her, sniffing at her bent head and she sat up straighter. "What should I do?" she asked him. "Just give up on Dad and go dancing off into the desert with Miguel?" Cody whined and nuzzled her hand.

"I can't!" She stood abruptly and Cody rubbed his head against her leg. "I'll never know what it is I feel about Miguel until I know what happened to Dad. There *has* to be something else I can do to find him. There *has* to be."

She paced forward a few steps, then turned and retraced them. Back and forth she went. Cody sat and watched her, moving his head from side to side to follow her.

Forcing herself to concentrate, she listed her options. One, she could reexamine the area already searched in the hope of stumbling upon a clue someone else had missed. Two, she could expand the grid Sergeant Kelly had drawn around the camp and explore new areas. Three, she could go over her father's belongings yet another time. Would his truck and his contents be released to her? she wondered.

If only she could find his journals. They might contain notes revealing his plans or the direction he was going to take.

Four, she could place her own ad in the local papers. Although the official publicity promised anonymity, someone might be more willing to talk to her than to the police. Five...

Her mind went blank and she sighed. She didn't have a five. Her first two were time-consuming and probably hopeless. And she'd already studied her father's belongings twice.

That left number four, even if the expense of advertising and offering a reward would deplete her rainy-day savings. Finding her father was worth any price.

But she needed to take immediate action; she couldn't bring herself to drive back into town to place the ad, then sit and wait. Then she'd have to think about Miguel and his declaration of love. And she couldn't think about that. She simply didn't have the room inside her head.

Neither could she bear to stay here and stare at what had once been her father's camp. "C'mon, Cody," she said, striding toward the jeep. She'd go back and talk to Hank, she decided. He'd led her to this place. If she prodded his memory, he might think of something else.

CODY RECOGNIZED his surroundings as Dusty drove down the winding road to Hank's cabin. He stood up on all fours and pushed his nose against the windshield, smearing the glass. Smoke was rising from the chimney when Dusty pulled to a stop, but the door was closed. Cody scrambled out of the jeep and tore around the side of the cabin.

Following, Dusty saw Hank shoveling dirt onto a long, wooden box topped with a screen. Barking excitedly, Cody rushed to him and Hank dropped the shovel to hug him.

"'Bout time you showed up," Hank told her. "Thought you done forgot me." He peered over her shoulder. "So where's that Happy Jack? Makin' hisself at home by my fire and eating my beans?"

Dusty shook her head. The tears she'd repressed since Sergeant Kelly had terminated the official search swelled within her. "Can't find him," she rasped through her dry throat.

"But . . ." Hank glanced down at the dog where forepaws still rested on his chest, then back at Dusty. "Let's go inside and have some coffee," he said, extricating himself. He grasped Dusty by the elbow and led her to his front door. Once inside, he sat her down at the small table and pulled out two battered tin cups. An equally battered coffeepot sat on the back of the wood stove. Using a frayed dish towel as a hot pad, he picked up the pot and poured a thick, black liquid into the cups.

Joining her at the table, he set a cup in front of her, then pulled an unlabeled brown bottle from a shelf and added a dollop of amber fluid to the steaming brew. "Drink up and get a hold of yourself. I'll listen when you're ready."

Dusty eyed the steaming brew with misgiving, but obediently brought the cup to her lips. She smelled coffee laced with cinnamon and other spices she couldn't identify. She took a tiny sip, then another. Flavored with an extraordinary spiced brandy, it was the best espresso she'd ever tasted.

Hank grinned, visibly pleased by her surprise. "Like my coffee strong," he said, "and I brew my own grog. Not that I don't mind some good store-bought from time to time."

Dusty set down her cup. "I didn't know I was coming, or I would've brought some."

"Don't seem like we got nothing to celebrate," he said. "How come you got Cody here—" he glanced at the dog lying at his feet "—and not Jack?"

After another fortifying sip of the espresso, Dusty told him her story. "'Tain't right," he muttered when she'd finished. "'Tain't right at all." He got up to replenish their drinks, then sat down again.

He blew noisily upon the hot liquid, scratched at his stubbled cheeks, ran a hand through his unkempt hair and screwed up his lined face as he thought. Dusty waited. With no place else to turn, she figured she had all day.

"Bet it was those gents from Utah!" he exclaimed suddenly, slamming his open hand on the table so hard that Cody jumped up and ran to the door. "No, you ain't going out there to chase my chickens," Hank told him.

"What men from Utah?"

"The ones with the bad whiskey," Hank said darkly. "I done told you when you was here before. Made me so sick, I plumb lost all track of my days."

He had, she remembered, mentioned something about bad whiskey, but, in a hurry to get to work and thinking he was going to spin some alcohol-inspired yarn or other, she'd cut him off.

"You think these men have something to do with my father?" she asked. Her heart began to thump in her chest, but she struggled to keep calm and not hope for too much.

"They was askin' about him, said they was his buddies and needed to find him. I didn't think they looked none too friendly, kinda squinty-eyed and shifty, so all

I said was I'd seed him but didn't know where he'd gone." He patted his pockets absently as he talked, then paused when he found his tin of chewing tobacco and pulled out a pinch.

"What did they look like?"

"Big, but soft, running to fat, you know? Younger 'n Jack, forties or so. Two dark-haired, one light. One of 'em had a big ugly scar down his cheek." He ran a hand down the right side of his own face. "He was right nasty-looking and started mumbling 'bout helping me remember. I was durned glad I had old Betsy with me." He waved his hand at the old rifle mounted on the wall.

"The light-haired one seemed to be the boss. Told the scar to shut up and acted real nice. Said he had real good news for Jack and was anxious to share it with 'im. It was gettin' nigh on dark and he asked if I'd mind if they camped here for the night. Be glad to share their dinner with me, had some nice juicy steaks in their cooler."

He stopped to wet his throat with the cooling coffee. "I didn't know what to think by then. Didn't seem right to send 'em away if they was friends of Jack's. So I said yes, figuring I'd get a better feel for 'em, then decide whether or not to say where I thought he was."

"What were their names?" Dusty asked, unable to stop herself.

Hank scratched his head. "Damned if I remember. Like I said before, they done offered me some whiskey, too, and I passed out like a light. Throwed up all the next day and took to my bed. Had to go to town to find out what day it was once I got better."

"You told them where you thought he was?"

Hank nodded. "Same as I told you. They said he was wastin' his time prospecting. Had some real money for him in Moab."

Dusty sat bolt upright in her chair. "Moab? You're sure they said Moab?"

"Sure as I'm sitting here. That's where you was, ain't it? Jack done told me about you being a tour guide and all, and I knew he was planning to go there, so when they said Moab, I figgered they was legit."

"When did they come?"

"Let's see." Hank stood and shuffled to a calendar hung near his bed. "I like to keep track of my days, so's I don't go into town to sell my gold and find the shop closed." He flipped back a page and then another. "Right around here," he said, pulling the thumbtack from the wall and bringing the calendar to the table.

"Last week in August," he explained, pointing. "When I finally got out of bed, the twenty-fifth was the last day crossed off and when I got my strength back and went to town, I found out it was the twenty-ninth."

Piece by piece, things were falling into place. "Did you go to a doctor?"

"I done got better, didn't need to pay no doctor to tell me so."

"But what if they poisoned you and it's still in your system?" she worried.

"By the time I quit throwing up, there wasn't nothing left!" Hank cackled. "I may be old, but I'm a tough old horse. Had some pretty strange dreams, though, I recollect. Thought it was the fever at the time. You think those three done took Jack somewheres?"

Dusty nodded. "He knows the canyons around Moab like the back of his hand," she said slowly, "and they took his journals, too."

"Why wouldn't they take his truck? Thought it was a right good one myself."

"Dad's been in and out of Moab for years in that truck. Someone could recognize it. They'd have to at least get rid of the wooden camper he made."

"So what's in Moab?"

"Indian ruins. There's a big black market for authentic artifacts. Dad loved to explore, but he always left the sites the way he found them. Someone with less respect and more greed could make a lot of money if they knew where they were."

"You reckon they done kidnapped him?"

Dusty nodded and stood, expression grim. "I'd never have thought someone would come to Arizona to get him, but that has to be what happened. There's no way Dad would ever willingly help pothunters. He calls them pillagers of the past."

She hugged Hank, thanked him for the information and promised to bring Jack back for a visit. Then she rushed Cody back to her truck. Ignoring the dog's whine of protest at the bouncing ride across the meadow, she drove as fast as she dared, slowing only when she reached the narrow, hairpin curves leading up and out of the canyon.

At last she had a clue to her father's whereabouts. He was alive, she was certain, because the kidnappers would need him to decipher his journals. She couldn't wait to share the news with Miguel and drove straight to his house.

The door was locked and he didn't answer her knock. She stared at the closed door stupidly for a moment. She'd never considered the possibility that he wouldn't be home. Ever since she'd told him about her father, he'd stood by her side, ready to help and comfort.

Frustrated, she pounded on the door, then gave up and crossed to the flower box where he'd told her he kept his spare key. She didn't have time to search the town for him; she'd have to wait until she saw him at work. Letting herself in, she walked up the stairs and packed her clothes.

MIGUEL WAS COUNTING MONEY and putting it into the cash register behind the bar when Dusty arrived at La Margarita. She called his name and saw him turn, his face a mask. Her eagerness to see him wilted into uncertainty.

"I think I know where my father is." He cocked an eyebrow and waited. "Remember the old miner I told you about who first told me where to look for Dad?" He nodded, and she blurted out the rest of her story, but his impassive expression didn't alter.

"And I suppose you're going to rush up to Moab and find him on your own?" he asked when she was done.

"I have the best idea where he'd take them, where they couldn't use bulldozers and really wreck the place."

He studied her a moment, his lips thinning with an air of disapproval. "I guess there's nothing to say except good luck, then." He turned back to the cash register and resumed filling the till.

Dusty gaped at his back. This was love? "Fine," she snapped. "I'll go tell Mamá Rosa I'm leaving."

She found her in the kitchen, putting the final touches on a stew she'd made for their dinner. *"Mi hija,"* Mamá Rosa protested, "surely you will not go alone? Miguel will go with you?"

Dusty evaded her worried gaze. "He doesn't seem to be speaking to me."

"¡Dios mío! At a time like this!" She bustled out of the kitchen. Dusty heard their voices rise, but they spoke in Spanish. A few minutes later, Mamá Rosa burst back through the swinging door.

"You are going to search alone? Not notify the police?" she asked.

"I don't have any proof and they'll waste time. The longer I wait, the worse the ruins will be desecrated." Mamá Rose began to shake her head ominously. "I won't try to rescue him by myself," Dusty assured her. "I have a good idea where he may have led them. I'll be careful and only go far enough to be sure I'm right, then I'll inform the authorities."

"And she'll take Cody with her." Miguel stood in the doorway. "See what I mean, Mamá? Nothing for us to worry about." His voice was ice-cold. "Shall we eat now?" Not waiting for an answer, he stepped back and let the door swing shut.

Mamá Rosa looked after him, then at Dusty and threw up her hands. Muttering to herself in Spanish, she picked up two hot pads and carried the stew into the dining room. She set the pot in the middle of the table with a thump.

Miguel took a seat on the opposite side of the table from Dusty. His withdrawal hit her with force. His easygoing nature, she realized, was slow to anger, but once sparked burned deeply.

She had to go through her story a third time when Carmen, Luisa, the busboys and the dishwashers joined them. "I called Ramona this afternoon," she said, turning to Mamá Rosa when she'd finished. "She has a friend at school looking for a job, and they'll both come in tomorrow so Mona can train her." She paused and chewed her lower lip. "I really do apologize for leaving like this."

Mamá Rosa reached out and patted her hand. "Do not worry, we will be all right. A child must be loyal to her father, but please, I beg you, do not go alone. This is a matter for the police, not a young girl."

"I know those canyons like the back of my hand. The men who have my father will never know I'm there." Unable to stop herself, she glanced at Miguel, who'd glowered at her throughout the meal.

"She is a liberated lady, Mamá," he said. "She does not need us or our advice. She needs no one." He turned back to Dusty. "Excuse me," he pretended to apologize, "I mean woman, not lady."

Dusty grabbed her glass of milk and sipped it, hoping to hide her face, to hide the hurt slicing through her. "If I recall," she said, setting down her glass, "you defined a lady as a woman who enjoyed her femininity, and I believe I learned that lesson well."

She paused, letting her steady gaze remind him of how he'd taught her to enjoy her body, to enjoy the difference between the sexes. "I wasn't aware that a lady also had to learn how to *obey* a man."

"What would you have her do, Miguel?" Carmen asked, as he glared at Dusty.

"Stay in his bed," Luisa answered for him.

Miguel scowled at his sisters. "I would have her exercise common sense and show some consideration for those who—" he paused "—care for her." He shoved himself away from the table and stood, picking up his barely touched bowl of stew. "Even if she can't return—" he paused again "—their feelings." He strode away.

Dusty bolted to her feet. "If you truly care for someone," she yelled at his back, "then you respect her abilities and don't try to tell her what to do!" Miguel stiffened, but he did not turn.

Her anger dissipating as quickly as it had risen, Dusty sank back into her chair. "Do not worry," Mamá Rosa said, "*Mi Miguelito* will calm down. He is stubborn and proud." She smiled softly. "Just like his father."

Dusty managed a smile and kept her doubts to herself. But the tension escalated throughout the evening. She dreaded going to the bar for drinks; her heart twisted in pain every time Miguel looked at her.

Finally the last customers left and the restaurant closed. Mamá Rosa and her daughters hugged Dusty and bade her good-bye. "You will come back?" the older woman asked.

"I don't know," she murmured, moving toward Miguel. He saw her coming but didn't move from behind the bar. She gazed at him helplessly, not knowing what to say. Remaining silent, she committed his features to memory. His silky black hair and high forehead. Large eyes, so dark, they were almost black. The straight nose, the fine cut of his mouth, the tiny cleft in his chin.

"I suppose you'll need to get your clothes," he said.

She shook her head. "I picked them up this afternoon." She wished she hadn't. If they were alone in his home, maybe he would relent. Maybe they could at least part as friends.

"I guess this is good-bye, then."

Dusty blinked. How could he have said he loved her only that morning and now dismiss her so coldly? "Th-thank you," she stuttered, "for everything." But she didn't move. She stood and looked at him, silently begging for a glimpse of the warm, tender, yet passionate Miguel she'd come to know. But the impersonal face of a stranger stared back at her and she finally turned, her movements slow, the pain she felt seeming to bruise her whole body, a pain that increased with each step she put between Miguel and her.

DUSTY DROVE HOME. Let Cody out of the apartment, where she'd left him before going to work, and walked him around the yard on a leash, the leash she'd bought with Miguel. Took the dog back inside. Packed up her camping equipment and loaded the Willys with everything she owned, save for the clothes she would don in the morning and the foam pad and sleeping bag that made up her bed. Last, she wrote a note to her landlord, informing him she wouldn't be renewing her lease.

And then she fell into bed, snuggling up to Cody and wishing he were Miguel, but sleep failed to come to her rescue. Now she wished she hadn't been so efficient in planning her early-morning departure and had left the dog at Miguel's house. She longed for an excuse to go to him. There'd been something unfinished, something unsaid in their parting....

The pain swelled within her until she could no longer hold it inside. She cried. Cried for the man whose love she'd lost before she'd recognized her own love for him.

Cody wriggled closer, shifting to bring his head to hers, and his warm, wet tongue licked at the salt on her cheeks. "What have I done?" she asked the dog. "But what else could I do?" She couldn't just call and ask the Canyonlands Park Service personnel to go looking for her father. Even if they were willing to go, she could barely begin to explain how to get to the site her father had described when they'd planned their birthday backpacking trip.

Dusty was sure that was the site he'd chosen. Its inaccessibility would allow him to appear cooperative, yet limit the pothunters operation without endangering his own life.

She knew she was right. Knew, too, that she could hike into the canyon and back out again without being detected. If only Miguel would understand and trust her. If only he would still love her....

She could locate her father, then return to Pinecreek and try to renew her relationship with Miguel, but what was the use? As she'd thought from the beginning, theirs was an attraction of opposites with no room for compromise. His good-bye had been final.

As hers must be.

No matter that he'd argued against her continuing her search and going to Utah alone out of love and concern for her safety. Those reasons were simply dressed-up versions of wanting her to do as she was told. And she couldn't live that way. She had to do what *she* believed was right.

But it hurt to leave him...to know she'd never again see his smile...hear his melodic voice...his warm body next to hers....

She rocked back and forth, moaning Miguel's name. She'd sympathized with Wayne when Rachel had left, but hadn't truly understood how he'd felt.

Now she did.

When she got to Moab, she would go to Wayne's, she decided. As he'd cried on her shoulder, she would cry on his. And she would learn to live without Miguel.

She woke with puffy, red-rimmed eyes, feeling not at all rested, but dragged herself out of bed and took Cody downstairs to the yard. She yawned and blindly followed him when he tugged on his leash. She'd hoped the crisp morning air would clear her foggy head, but when Cody finished visiting every bush in the yard, she felt no better.

She took her shower and fed the dog, but felt little appetite herself. Gathering up her sleeping gear, she looked about the empty room, remembering the night Miguel had brought her home and listened so sympathetically to her story. Taking a deep, steadying breath, she firmly walked out the door.

"Heel," she commanded Cody, needing him to stay on her left so she wouldn't trip on the leash. He obeyed until she reached the Willys, when he suddenly lunged at the old jeep. Barking loudly, he propped his front paws against the door. Dusty could barely see around her rolled-up pad and sleeping bag. "Shh," she said irritably. "Get down. I have to open the door." She fumbled with the key, trying to unlock the door with one hand, while her other balanced her belongings on one hip.

The door opened of its own accord. Miguel tumbled out, his hair mussed, his eyes still clouded with sleep and her spare key in his hand. Her arms went limp and sleeping pad and bag rolled beneath the truck.

He grinned and she threw herself into his welcoming embrace. Words tumbled out of her mouth, but her joy made her incoherent. She'd never thought to see him look at her again with that light in his eyes, never thought to see him at all, much less feel his arms around her.

Then he kissed her and her futile efforts to make sense ceased altogether. "I am sorry, *mi corazón*," he said when he raised his head. "I acted like a child, a cruel child." He studied her smiling face for a moment. "You are happy to see me?"

"Yes!" She hugged him again, then said simply, "I love you. I know that now."

Uttering a whoop, he lifted her into the air and spun her in circles. She dropped Cody's leash, but he leaped up with them, eager to partake in their game. Miguel set Dusty back upon the ground, then retrieved the leash.

"And I love you," he said, slipping a loop in the leash onto his wrist and linking his fingers behind her waist.

"And I will try to learn, as Mamá says, to accept you as you are—infuriatingly independent. Perhaps you will try to lean on me a little more?"

She nodded hesitantly, afraid he would ask her not to go to Moab, but his next words contained quite a different message. "Then you have no objection to me continuing to help you search for your father?"

"Oh, Miguel!" Pleased by his offer, yet worried because he knew little of the rigors of backcountry travel, she felt happy and sad all at the same time. "What about work?" she asked, stalling for time.

"Mamá says they will manage without me. Both Carmen and Luisa's husbands fill in from time to time." His familiar grin appeared. "And she said that without you, I will wear a long face and scare the customers away." He brushed her cheek with his lips. "As usual, she's right."

Dusty hid her face in his shoulder while she thought about his proposal. He might be inexperienced, but was in excellent physical shape. The prospect of Miguel joining her made her look at the situation in a different light. She suddenly understood why he'd been so angry with her.

She lifted her head. "I couldn't bear it if something happened to you, Miguel," she finally said, unable to hide her worry.

"The boot is on the other foot, eh?" he asked, his grin telling her he'd guessed what she was thinking.

"You have to promise to listen to me," she warned him. "I'm sure I can borrow equipment for you from my friends, but you have to rest when I say rest, drink water when I say drink. Hiking in the backcountry is serious business."

"Bossy as well as infuriatingly independent," he said cheerfully. "Shall we go?" He stepped away from the driver's door and ushered her into the seat. He retrieved her bedroll and pad from under the truck and loaded them, as well as Cody, into the back. Not happy with his answer and wanting to impress upon him the importance of her experience, Dusty waited without starting the engine.

"If you slow me down, I'll leave you behind," she bluffed when he climbed into the passenger seat.

"No, you won't," he assured her. "You love me."

"I'm not sure I know much about this love business," she muttered, but turned the key in the ignition.

"Love means we'll get married after we find your father, have babies and live happily ever after."

About to pull out of the driveway, Dusty slammed on the brakes. "Where?" she asked, turning to face him. He looked at her blankly. "Where would we live?" Her voice rose, in pain rather than anger. "Are you willing to leave your family, home and restaurant and stay in Utah with me?"

The surprise and consternation on his handsome face gave her his answer before he spoke. "I'm more than a bartender, Dusty. I help Mamá run that restaurant, and someday it will be mine—and my children's. How can I leave?"

"I know." She stared straight out the windshield, letting her shoulders slump. "This isn't going to work."

"Would living here in Pinecreek be so awful?" he asked after a moment of silence.

"Not initially,"she admitted. "But year after year? I'm not so sure." His dark eyes seemed to reflect her own misery. "You want a traditional wife, Miguel, content with home and hearth. I left that life when I left my mother's at eighteen. I'm used to being on my own, coming and going as I please, moving with the seasons. I love you, but . . ."

"Hush." He pressed his forefinger against her lips. "First comes love, and the rest we'll work out. We'll take one step at a time, okay?"

"Yes." Heartened by his patience, she took his hand between both of hers and planted a kiss upon his palm. Her own eyes downcast, she didn't see the shadows in his.

DURING THE LONG DRIVE to Moab, Miguel paid scant attention to the changing scenery. They ascended into the ponderosa pine country of Flagstaff, then passed through the Navajo reservation in the northeast corner of Arizona. Dusty pointed out Monument Valley and he obediently admired the famous Mittens and the other rock formations that rose so unexpectedly from the flat ground, but he concentrated on figuring out the woman he loved.

She was a product of extreme opposites. Carefree summers with her father stood in sharp contrast to the duty-laden school months with her mother. Twelve years older than the first of three stepsisters born in six years, Dusty had come home from school to help her mother clean, cook and care for her babies.

"Every spring Mom would lay a guilt trip on me," Dusty told him. "How could I leave her to spend the summer with Jack when she needed me so much?" Her lips twisted with the bitterness of memory as she spoke. "She enjoyed caring for her home and wanted me to enjoy it too. Wanted me to be more like her—but I wasn't and I'm not.

"Every time I got on the plane to go back East, I felt like I was returning to prison."

"Don't you think caring for *our* home and *our* children would be different than caring for your mother's?"

Dusty chewed her lip. "That's what my mother always said."

"And you know I'm quite capable of doing my share of the cooking and cleaning," he added.

"I know, Miguel," she said quietly. "I want to be with you, I really do." She glanced at him, then returned her attention to the road, but not before he'd seen her haunted expression. "But what if I start to feel trapped? I'd be miserable and make you miserable, too. And then we'd hate one another. Look what happened to my parents. Dad tried to settle down, but he just wasn't capable of it."

"You're not your father."

"No, but we're very much alike."

Miguel fell silent, not knowing what else to say. Understanding Dusty's reservations about marriage brought him no closer to winning her over to his point of view. But he wasn't about to give up. He loved this sexy, free-spirited woman and was determined to persuade her to settle in Pinecreek.

But how?

12

MIGUEL HADN'T ANSWERED that question by the time they crossed into Utah and drove into the higher elevations of Bluff and Blanding, then down into the red rock country of Moab. Dusty pulled to a stop in front of a tiny brick house on the outskirts of town. She beeped the horn and a man burst through the door. She hopped out, ran up the walk and he swept her into a bear hug.

Miguel got out of the Willys more slowly. The man wasn't much older than he was and he felt a flash of jealousy at the sight of him hugging his woman. Dusty turned and beckoned. "Miguel," she said excitedly, "I want you to meet Wayne Landis. He's a former river runner who got his college degree and now he's an archaeologist with the Bureau of Land Management."

The man had curling black hair and piercing blue eyes. Although no taller than Miguel, he was huskier. He glanced at Dusty, then offered his hand. "Never thought I'd see the day a man put a smile like that on Dusty's face."

His grip was strong and firm, his pleasure apparently genuine, and Miguel's jealousy had faded by the time he released his hand. "I've known this little brat since the day she was born and had the dubious pleasure of babysitting her more often than I like to remember," Wayne continued. "As her unofficial big brother, I have to ask if your intentions are honorable."

His lips smiled, but the sharpness of his blue eyes belied the humor in his tone. "More honorable than she likes," Miguel answered. "I intend to marry her."

Wayne flicked a glance at Dusty's uneasy expression and nearly bent double with laughter. Dusty punched Wayne in the arm, but Miguel refused to crack a smile. Regaining control of himself, Wayne extended his hand again. "I wish you the very best of luck in taming this hellion."

"If we're finished with the male bonding," Dusty observed dryly, "could we go inside and let me explain why we're here?"

Wayne led Miguel into the house, while Dusty fetched Cody and put him in the fenced backyard. When each of them had a beer, and Wayne had found some steaks in his freezer to thaw in his microwave oven, they settled at the table in the windowed nook that served as his dining room.

Wayne frowned as Dusty related her story. "I'm not so sure it's pots they're after," he said when she'd finished. "Dinosaur bones are claiming higher prices right now. There's a shop in Moab that sells a ton a month."

"You go into the stores?" Miguel asked, surprised.

"Unofficially. I can't do anything without proof that the bones were taken from public lands or without a private owner's permission, but I like to remind them that the BLM is keeping an eye on them." The line of his mouth was grim.

"Dad's always been fascinated by the Anasazi, though," Dusty argued. "He may have run across some fossil sites, but he knows the ruins best."

"Still could be the same ring," Wayne mused aloud. "Maybe the heat we've been putting on the bone shops is making them switch back to pothunting."

Dusty kept silent while Wayne thought. "Jack mentioned a find in the Needles district before he left for Pinecreek. He was going to show me when he got back."

"Salt Creek Canyon," she confirmed.

Wayne shook his head. "That's one of the most popular trails in the district. If anyone were excavating, they'd have been seen and reported by now."

"Some of the side canyons have tributaries of their own," Dusty countered, "and where there's water, there could be cliff dwellings."

"There aren't any roads into those side canyons," Wayne shot back.

"All the better," Dusty insisted. "Their only worry would be if the rare backpacker stumbled across them."

Apparently convinced, Wayne stood and ducked into an adjoining room, then returned with a map and spread it over the table. Miguel had never seen anything like it. It was, he determined from the legend in the lower left corner, a topographical map. He continued to listen quietly while Dusty and Wayne argued over which side canyon Jack would have chosen. Dusty, he noted, conceded no more to Wayne than she ever did to him.

Growing hungry, and unable to contribute anything to the conversation, Miguel offered to make dinner.

Wayne lifted his head from the map long enough to point him to the back door, where the grill was, and he set to work. By the time the coals were ready, he'd found potatoes to bake and the makings for salad.

"I'll give you six days," Wayne was saying when Miguel brought loaded plates to the table.

"That's barely enough time to check a side trail or two!" Dusty protested.

"Six days." Wayne looked at Miguel as he sat down. "The canyons make radio contact impossible, so I need to know when to expect you back," he explained. "It's a half day's drive in and a half day out, which leaves five full days for hiking. Six days, or I send the Park Service in after you."

"Sounds good to me," Miguel agreed.

"A week," Dusty insisted and scowled at both men. Wayne conceded. They ate in silence for a few minutes, then Wayne asked Dusty if she'd had the Willys checked recently.

"I had some trouble with the carburetor while I was in Pinecreek," she admitted, "but that's fixed and it's been fine ever since."

"Take my truck," Wayne said. "I don't want you to risk breaking down with pothunters in the area."

"The jeep is fine." Miguel spoke up. "I had my mechanic go over it while it was in his garage."

"You what?" Dusty's tone was incredulous rather than grateful and Miguel winced. Rather than pleasing her, he'd again stepped on her prickly independence again.

"How much do I owe you?" Dusty asked, her voice cold.

"The bill's at home. I really don't remember." Looking down at his plate, he hacked at the tender steak, mangling it into shreds.

"Why don't you just say thank-you?" Wayne asked Dusty. "The man did you a favor. What's the big deal?"

Dusty pushed her plate away, leaving her dinner half-eaten. "This is why I can't marry him. He seems to think I need a keeper. When Willys wouldn't start, I figured it might be the carburetor. I could've had it towed and fixed, but he went ahead and made the arrangements without consulting me. Now he turns around and has it checked out without even telling me!"

"So?" Wayne asked as Miguel exhaled explosively.

"So I can take care of my car myself!"

"But you didn't," Wayne reminded her. "And it was due for a checkup before you rushed down to Pine-creek."

Dusty threw up her hands. "Okay, okay!" She shoved her chair away from the table and stood. "I figured I'd find Dad and we'd give the engine an overhaul together, but I didn't find him and I was too cheap to pay a mechanic. Are you satisfied?"

She picked up her plate and stalked to the kitchen, but not before Miguel saw tears glistening in her eyes. She was still wound up, he realized, taut with tension and worry over her father and the future of their relationship. He got to his feet.

"Go easy on her," Wayne advised and Miguel paused. "Even as a kid, she always wanted to do things herself. She'd trip over her shoelaces all day rather than let anyone tie them for her."

Miguel grinned. "I believe it."

"You do know that if you get her to walk down that aisle, she's not going to turn into Susie Homemaker?"

"I'm not looking for maid service." Miguel's smile faded. "We both have some compromises to make, but we'll work them out."

Wayne studied him, then nodded. "I believe you will." Miguel returned his steady gaze, silently thanking him for the equally unspoken approval.

"You wouldn't happen to have any sisters with that attitude, would you?" Wayne asked, lightening the mood.

"Two are already taken and the third's only twenty-one."

"Too young." Wayne shook his head and feigned a hangdog expression. "I'd like to find a woman who knows the meaning of the word 'compromise.'"

Despite Wayne's attempt at levity, Miguel sensed truth—and bitterness—in his words. "If you're still free in a few years, I'll tell Mona to give you a call."

"Yeah, do that."

Miguel nodded and moved toward the kitchen. Dusty stood by the sink, her head bowed. He called her name softly and she whirled.

"What do you want?" she demanded. "An apology? My undying gratitude?" Her voice shook and she took a deep breath. "Okay, I admit it. I screwed up and you saved the day. Thank you."

Ignoring the anger and sarcasm in her tone, Miguel crossed the room and pulled her into his arms. "I don't want any of those things," he told her. He wanted her to lean on him, he added silently, to admit she needed him so that they could be a team, a couple, husband and wife, united for life.

"I think you need to rest," he said instead. "It's been a long day." He cupped the back of her head and brought it to rest upon his shoulder, then used both hands to rub her back. She relaxed against him.

"I don't deserve you," she said quietly. "I'm sorry I flew off the handle. It was nice of you to have your mechanic check out Willys."

"You're welcome." Miguel kissed the top of her head. Maybe they had a chance.

THEY ROSE BEFORE DAWN. Dusty had reluctantly admitted her tiredness and they'd gone straight to bed. Wayne got up with them, but it was obvious he'd stayed up later. He'd laid out food supplies on the kitchen counter, some fresh but most freeze-dried, and filled their water bottles. His sleeping bag, foam pad and backpack sat by the door.

"Did you bring a warm coat?" he asked Miguel, who was transferring clothes from his haphazardly packed suitcase to the backpack. "It gets pretty chilly when the sun goes down." Miguel showed him his leather bomber jacket, but Wayne declared it too bulky to wear under a backpack. He loaned him a lightweight, waterproof jacket as well as a cotton knit, long-sleeved T-shirt to be worn under his own flannel shirts and sweaters.

"The secret of keeping warm is layers," Wayne told him, then eyed his feet. "Those tennis shoes aren't sturdy enough for prolonged walking, especially over rocks."

Wayne's hiking boots were a size too large, but with an extra pair of socks, they fitted well enough. Lastly, Wayne offered him a revolver. Miguel stared at it with horrified fascination. He'd never touched a gun before, much less fired one.

"I've got my .22 in the Willys," Dusty said.

"That's fine for shooting rabbits," Wayne said gruffly. "You might have to stop something larger. Take the .357." Dusty took it and stuffed it into her backpack.

"You know how to handle that?" Miguel asked, when Wayne handed her a box of ammunition.

Dusty nodded. "My father taught me. A gun in the backcountry is a safety precaution, but I've never had to use one."

Yet, Miguel silently amended. *You've never gone looking for criminals before.* He turned away. He believed the benefit of possessing a gun was outweighed by the possibility of having it used against him, but couldn't bring himself to object to taking it. He could only pray they wouldn't have to use it.

They said good-bye to Cody, because Wayne, worried the dog might scent Jack and reveal their presence, insisted on keeping him. Dusty had wanted to take him, hoping he'd speed up the search, but Miguel had added his argument to Wayne's, and for once she'd relented.

They finished loading the jeep and Dusty climbed behind the steering wheel. "If something doesn't look right, turn around," Wayne advised. "Don't get any ideas about rescuing Jack. Come back and report pothunters and I'll get the BLM and the Park Service out in force."

Wholeheartedly agreeing, Miguel shook Wayne's hand, then slid into the passenger seat. Dusty's agreement was less enthusiastic as she started the engine.

"One week," Wayne called after them, "or I'm sending the troops after you!"

AS THEY HEADED SOUTH, retracing part of their route into town, Dusty gave Miguel her tour guide speech. Moab lay in a valley of rolling desert, studded with eroded sandstone outcroppings and ringed by the pine-strewn La Sal Mountains on the east, the Abajos to the south, the Henrys to the southwest and, far to the north, the multicolored rock formations topped with trees called the Bookcliffs. When they passed Wilson Arch, located along the highway, she boasted that it only hinted at the spectacular beauties found in Arches National Park north of Moab.

"Once Dad is safe and sound, we'll take you on a tour of the area. If you have time before—"

"Before I go home?" he finished for her. "What about us?"

Dusty glanced at him, then returned her attention to the road, glad that they were approaching their turn-off. She flicked on her right directional signal and made the turn with extreme care to avoid looking at the hurt in Miguel's eyes.

"I don't know," she replied. As much as she loved Miguel, her return to this rocky canyon country intensified her doubts about settling in Pinecreek. She'd seen her parents' relationship deteriorate into bitterness and hatred and couldn't bear to see that happen to Miguel and her.

She'd rather walk away and preserve the memory of their love.

To block out such painful thoughts, she resumed pointing out the sights they were passing. Newspaper Rock, a fifty-foot-high stone face covered with petroglyphs and fenced off from the damaging fingers of tourists, rock climbers hugging the towering walls of Indian Creek Canyon, and Dugout Ranch, one of the earliest and largest cattle ranches in the Southwest.

To her delight, Miguel took an avid interest and asked questions. He was, she suspected, as eager as she to avoid thinking about their future. As they approached the southern entrance to Canyonlands, the sight of the familiar orange- and white-banded cliffs of the Needles district made her smile, a smile that widened when she heard Miguel suck in his breath at the sight.

She pulled to the side of the road, allowing him time to absorb the vista of ancient sandstone eroded into a maze of canyons topped by fins and ridges, domes and spires, arches and windows in a display of natural architecture that bore an uncanny resemblance to a city skyline.

"Kind of makes you appreciate the power of nature," she said dryly. Miguel nodded, apparently struck dumb. "Canyonlands is almost a half million acres," she told him, pleased by his silent appreciation. "The Colorado and Green Rivers divide the park into three districts. The Needles lies to the east of their confluence, while the Maze is to the west." She pointed to their right. "Island in the Sky lies to the north, between both rivers, and overlooks the entire park."

They stopped at the Needles Outpost to fill up on gas and at the Visitor Information Center to pay their park fee and obtain a backcountry permit. When they left the pavement behind, they crossed rolling sage flats on a graded dirt road for several miles, the convoluted cliff walls ahead beckoning. Then Dusty turned off the road and they entered Salt Creek Canyon.

Their trail crisscrossed the twisting wash bottom of the shallow stream. Deciduous trees and shrubs tinged with autumnal hues of gold and scarlet crowded the streambed, while evergreen juniper and piñon struggled for footholds in the orange-red canyon walls.

Miguel gasped when the trail came to an end at a deep section of the stream. A steep, heavily treed bank formed the opposite side. "Did we make a wrong turn?" he asked, sure they'd reached a dead end but not wanting to insult Dusty by suggesting they were lost.

Dusty shook her head and pressed the accelerator, turning right and plowing up the middle of the creek. Water splashed into their open windows. "Don't slow down!" Miguel shouted; he felt mud suck at the tires.

"Miguel," Dusty snapped, exasperation in her voice. "I do this for a living. Relax."

Miguel mumbled an apology. She was right; he was neither recognizing nor respecting her abilities. When he told her so, she flashed him a brilliant smile.

"Quicksand can be a problem, of course," she admitted, "but if we stick to the trail, we shouldn't hit any."

All the same, Miguel sighed with relief when Dusty guided the Willys out of the floorboard-deep water. Gradually he relaxed enough to laugh at himself whenever the trail crossed the stream and he caught himself glancing to his right, as though he expected another vehicle to be approaching the "intersection."

"I can see why the Anasazi chose to live here," he observed when Dusty pointed out the crumbling remains of Indian structures set in inconspicuous alcoves in the cliff walls.

"They had to use ladders to reach their farm plots on the canyon floor," Dusty pointed out, "and the women were the ones responsible for hauling up the water."

Miguel grinned. "The first feminists?"

Dusty smiled, but continued. "It was a communal society. Everyone worked and everyone shared in the results. Quite the opposite of what was going on in medieval Europe at the time—lords and ladies living off the labor of starving serfs."

"I never realized that—" Miguel broke off. Dusty had suddenly braked to a stop and jumped out of the truck. Following, he saw her standing by the blackened remains of a camp fire ringed with empty beer cans and littered with cigarette butts. Her face was red with outrage. "What's the matter?" he asked.

"The cardinal rule of the backcountry is to pack out whatever you pack in!" she exclaimed. "Even toilet paper. This is disgusting!" She marched to the truck and returned with a bag, and together they cleaned up the mess. Dusty paused to study one of the cigarette butts she'd picked up. Miguel peered over her shoulder.

"This was hand rolled," she told him. "See how the lip end is twisted? And there's no brand name." Miguel nodded and waited for her to explain. "Dad rarely

smokes, but when he does, he always rolls his own."
Growing pensive, she looked up the canyon.

"Would he litter?"

"Not normally. It's a long shot, but maybe he left it on purpose. He'd know I'd stop to pick up the mess." She dropped the butt into the bag and stood. "Let's go."

Miguel pulled the small cooler that contained their lunch from the back seat and they ate sandwiches while Dusty drove. Periodically they spotted the glint of sunlight on metal and stopped to find more of the same beer cans. Judging by their varying distance from the road, the two concluded they'd been tossed from a moving truck.

Dusty struggled not to get her hopes up. Not all backcountry travelers were as dedicated to leaving no sign of their passage as she was, and she figured pothunters would care less than most. A beer can wouldn't betray the criminal purpose of their trip, either.

"Let's try that side canyon," she said later, pointing one out.

"How do you know that's the one? It looks the same as a lot of the others we've seen."

"I don't," she admitted, "and I won't until we get into it, but we're over halfway in and the creek branches off into it." She stopped the truck and parked it off the trail.

"Where would they put their vehicle?" Miguel asked as they pulled their backpacks out of the jeep.

"They probably meet someone here on appointed days to pick up the pottery and bring them supplies." Dusty followed Miguel's pointed stare at the Willys. "Good thinking," she said, flushing slightly; she hadn't thought how obvious the jeep would be. "Guess we should park out of sight, up the trail."

THEY'D HIKED for several miles when Dusty cried out and pointed to a cliff above them. "See that sheer rock wall? Look at the petroglyph. The humpbacked flute player is Kokopelli, the god of fertility. You find him almost everywhere the Anasazi lived. The Navajo call him Watersprinkler. Dad mentioned that Kokopelli points the way to some ruins so far up a cliff and hidden by trees and shrubs, he didn't think anyone else had set foot in them."

"How did he find them?"

"Rock climbing." Dusty quickened her pace. "Keep an eye out for more. Dad said Kokopelli serves as a signpost."

Miguel was beginning to feel as humpbacked as Kokopelli, but, determined to show Dusty he could fit into her life, he kept going, although the straps of the pack rubbed at his shoulders and its length irritated his spine.

Dusty trudged ahead of him. Bent forward slightly, she carried her pack as though it were filled with tissue paper. He silently congratulated himself on not having offered to carry all the heavier items. She wouldn't have appreciated the gesture, and at that moment, he didn't think he could even bear the weight of an extra pair of socks.

His attention on the ground as he willed his feet to move, he almost plowed into Dusty when she called a halt. "Rest stop," she announced, her eyes twinkling when he immediately unfastened the backpack, removed it and sank to the ground. She kept her pack on and selected a rock for a seat then unhooked a canteen. "Drink," she commanded, waving a hand at his canteen.

"Don't fight the weight of the pack," she advised after they'd both drunk their fill and she'd helped him struggle back into it. "Bend with it and think of yourself as a gorilla. Lean forward and settle into a steady rhythm. You'll get used to it." She checked the straps and showed him how to adjust them to move the weight up or down his back for comfort.

Miguel beat his chest. "Me Tarzan, you Jane?" he asked hopefully.

"Later, baby," she promised with a smile and resumed walking.

Heartened, Miguel fell into step beside her. The repositioned pack no longer chafed his back and shoulders. "Have you noticed the cigarette butts on the trail?" he asked.

Dusty nodded. "I hate leaving them lie, but bending down with the packs on would slow us down and tire us out. Speaking of which, let's step it up. The sun goes down fast out here and I want to set up camp before dark."

"How far in are the ruins?" he asked, lengthening his stride.

"I'm not sure. If this is the right trail, I think Dad said close to two days."

They hiked for two more hours. Following Dusty's advice, Miguel tried to concentrate on putting one foot ahead of the other, but, interested in his surroundings, he kept looking up at the hawks and ravens soaring overhead. They frequently startled rabbits, squirrels and chipmunks. Once, to Miguel's awe, they came upon a group of desert bighorn sheep feeding at the base of a rubble slope. Even Dusty couldn't resist stopping to watch the rare animals.

They passed the blackened remains of another camp fire, again littered with cigarette butts, food wrappings and beer cans. This time they found an empty pouch of tobacco, the brand Jack Rose preferred, but Dusty refused to accept it as positive proof that they were on the right trail. Miguel thought it a good enough sign to call in the Park Service, but kept his mouth closed. He'd agreed to let her lead the expedition and she'd given him no reason to doubt her capabilities. Sensing that his agreement could affect their future together, he was determined to stick to it—unless she got a harebrained idea about rescuing her father. Then he'd ditch their packs and carry her out if necessary.

"They either got a later start than us or are moving slower," Dusty said, glancing at the sun, now low in the sky. "We've got a good hour of light left."

Again they set off. The shadows cast by the canyon walls grew deeper and longer before she called a stop at a spot where the stream curved around a cliff and left a large, dry patch of sand. Although signs indicated it was a designated camping site, they had the place to themselves.

The clear sky indicated that rain was unlikely, so rather than set up the tent, Miguel laid out their foam pads and unrolled the sleeping bags, while Dusty set up a tiny camp stove and boiled water from the stream.

Miguel stared sadly at the two sleeping bags, then began to search for firewood. He'd collected a large stack and set it near their bed when she called him to dinner.

"Freeze-dried beef and gravy," she told him. "But I dressed it up with spices, noodles and fresh vegetables."

"Delicious," Miguel said after his first few bites and meant it. The noodles, he supposed, were lighter to carry than potatoes and made the meal an interesting cross between stew and Stroganoff. They finished the water from their plastic bottles, then refilled them with boiled water.

"Time for a fire?" Miguel asked after they'd cleaned their few dishes, but Dusty shook her head.

"Why take the chance of being spotted? The ruins may be a good day's hike away. Let's just go to bed and get an early start tomorrow."

Miguel could barely contain his disappointment. They hadn't made love since they'd fought. Dusty had fallen asleep as soon as her head hit the pillow the previous night, and he hadn't had the heart to disturb her. "I'd like to at least hold you for a while before we sleep," he said simply.

Dusty smiled, but made no response; she crossed to their makeshift bed, knelt and unzipped her sleeping bag. Miguel frowned, thinking she'd ignored his request. But she moved to his bag and unzipped it, too.

"They're the same make," she explained, opening both. Laying one on top of the other, she zipped them back together. She'd barely finished before he tackled her and claimed her mouth in a deep, possessive kiss. To his delight, she responded readily and they were both breathing heavily when he raised his head.

"Let's get out of these clothes and under the covers," she said huskily and Miguel quickly complied. Despite their speed, the cool of the evening air chilled their bare flesh and they shivered when their bodies met, shivers that quickly turned to tremors as the heat of desire warmed them.

Miguel had meant to take her slowly, to show her with his touch how much he loved her. But the unfamiliar setting inflamed him. The starlight sky, framed by the dark shadows of the canyon walls . . . the pale, silvery gleam of the moon on Dusty's light hair . . . the rippling rush of the stream . . . the soughing of the breeze through the treetops . . . the lonely cry of a night bird . . . the chitter of crickets . . . the fresh fragrance of the outdoors, blending with the scent of Dusty's essence . . .

He felt primeval, drawn back to the roots of time when man's only concerns were those of survival— food, shelter, clothing—and the urge to procreate. The slow, tender lovemaking he conducted in his bedroom had no place here.

Here, he claimed his woman and demanded rather than wooed, filling his hands with the fullness of her breasts, then seeking the feminine warmth hidden between her legs . . . and taking, taking all she had to give.

Dusty gave with a ferocity that matched his own. She dug her fingers into his back and nipped at his shoulders with her teeth. When he cupped the curves of her buttocks, she wrapped her legs around his waist and met his thrust with an answering one of her own, needing him, welcoming him, drawing him deeper into herself.

Her hands on his hips, prodded him into a hard, driving rhythm that sent their senses spiraling beyond thought, narrowing their awareness to the joining of their rocking bodies until the whirl of sensation exploded into a cataclysm of ecstasy.

Unable to speak, Miguel could only moan, a moan he vaguely heard Dusty echo as their bodies stilled, the pleasure ebbing slowly, seeming to leave aftershocks like those that follow an earthquake.

"No, don't move," Dusty whispered, feeling him shift slightly.

"Don't worry," Miguel managed to mumble, "I can't." He felt the quiver of her laughter before she gave it voice, felt it in the rise and fall of her belly; he begged for mercy as he felt one last drop of pleasure seize him. And then he was laughing, too, and still wrapped together, they rolled from side to side.

"I didn't hurt you, did I?" he asked when he got his breath, knowing that his touch had bordered on roughness.

"If that was pain," Dusty said dryly, "I must be a masochist." She wriggled lower and planted a kiss upon his chest. "I love you, Miguel Santiago," she said and rested her head over the steadying beat of his heart.

"And I love you, Dusty Rose," he answered, but he stared at the starlight sky long after she slept. How could his modest home compete with the magnificence of these canyons?

13

MIGUEL QUESTIONED Dusty's authority for the first time the next afternoon. Examining another littered campsite, they found a compass, the same make as her father's, tucked inside the crumpled wrapper of a package of dehydrated soup. "It's sold in any sports store," Dusty insisted when Miguel suggested they turn back and call in the Park Service. "Just because he owns one doesn't mean it's his. Someone else could have dropped it."

"Why would it be inside a foil bag?"

"To protect it." She headed up the trail, ending the discussion.

"How much proof do you need?" Miguel persisted when he caught up with her. "At the rate we're going, we'll stumble into their camp and be captured before you're satisfied."

"I brought binoculars. We'll see them before they ever see us."

"Fat lot of good they're doing us in your pack."

"You agreed to follow my lead," she retorted. "If you want to turn back, go ahead!"

They glared at one another. "I am not leaving you alone!" he yelled. "But it's midafternoon and you said you thought it was a two-day hike to the ruins. Don't you think it's time to start exercising a little caution?"

"All right!" She flung off her pack and opened it. Rummaging inside, she pulled out her field glasses. "When we reach a bend in the trail, I'll use these before we go around it. Okay?"

"An excellent idea. I should have thought of it myself." Miguel grinned, pleased by her compromise, no matter how ungraciously she'd made it. She was still scowling, but he could see she had to work at it by the softening of the expression in her eyes.

They resumed their steady plodding. Leg muscles unused to supporting ninety pounds on Miguel's back had made themselves felt that morning, but the stiffness had gradually eased with exercise. As the day progressed, he found himself enjoying the solitude and understanding Dusty's enjoyment of backpacking. He felt as if they were the only people on earth, save for the jarring reminders of cigarette butts, which now offended him as much as they did her.

Dusty's bad temper had passed, he realized, when they reached a curve in the trail. She used the binoculars to peer around the corner with exaggerated care. Rather than take offense, he laughed with her.

"Any sign of Injuns up ahead?" he said in a stage whisper, shading his eyes with one hand and assuming a furtive stance.

"We're the Indians!" she whispered back, lowering the binoculars and beckoning to him to follow her. "You've seen too many cowboy movies," she added in a normal voice as they rounded the corner. "The white men are the bad guys in this show."

"I stand corrected," Miguel agreed easily and took her hand in his. With the sun beating down on him and the only sound the faint cawing of ravens overhead, he could almost forget what had brought him to this amazing country. But a sign Dusty spotted when she examined another section of trail provided a reminder that cast a shadow upon his light mood.

"It says the trail is closed," she said, peering through the binoculars, "but I can't read all of it. Let's take a closer look." She lowered the glasses and set off, but he grabbed her pack and brought her to an abrupt halt.

"Let me see," he demanded and she handed him the glasses. "It doesn't look official," he said, studying the sign. "I don't see any mention of the Park Service."

"Which is why we need to get closer."

"Just stop and think for a minute, will you?" Again Miguel shot out a hand to grasp her pack and hold her in place. "This could be the proof we need. Put yourself in the thieves' place. They'd have to do something to keep hikers from running across them. What better way than to play on the need for safety?"

"We can't be sure it's a fake without examining it more closely." She slapped at his arm to free herself, but Miguel shook her rather than let her go.

"The Park Service would know, if we went back and reported it."

"And what if it's their sign? We'd waste four days hiking back and forth!" Her mind was clearly made up, her chin jutting forward stubbornly.

Reluctantly he released her, his heartbeat accelerated with misgivings as he followed. The sign was obviously handmade, words scrawled in white paint on a piece of scrap lumber. Smaller print warned of a rock slide ahead, but they could see nothing through the field glasses other than more signs announcing the danger of loose rock.

"They don't look like park signs," Dusty said, "there's no insignia. Let's go a little farther and see if—"

"No." She must have heard the determination in his voice because she stared at him with a mixture of surprise and dismay. "You promised Wayne that you'd turn back and report anything suspicious," he reminded her. "We're not going any farther without getting help first."

She scowled at him, then turned to look at the rock walls. "I could climb up and see more from there."

Miguel followed her gaze. "Those cliffs go straight up. A bighorn couldn't climb them."

Dusty sighed. "I could with the right equipment, but I didn't bring it."

"So we go back?" he asked, not hiding his relief.

"Let me check the topo map and see how far we've come."

She pulled the map from a side pocket on her pack and selected a rock for a seat. Miguel paced restlessly and swung his arms to loosen his muscles. Looking up the canyon, he saw the sunlight catch on something shiny in the trees. A brief flash, he had to admit, but one he was sure didn't belong there. It had been the shimmer of light on metal . . . or glass.

Forcing himself to feign casualness, he stretched his back one last time, then returned to Dusty and squatted beside her. Gripping one side of the map and pretending to study it, he spoke calmly but forcefully.

"We're being watched. I saw the sun reflect on glass, probably binoculars." He felt it now, too. A sixth sense that he was sure was not his imagination made his exposed back prickle with awareness. Nothing in his backpack would deflect a bullet.

"Act disappointed and head back with me, but don't hurry."

She looked at him dubiously, but apparently his urgency convinced her. She nodded, then folded the map and tucked it away. Without further conversation they stood and set off at a slow, yet steady pace.

But when the trail twisted and turned, Dusty stopped short. "Are you sure you saw something or are you just trying to scare me into going back?"

"I saw something!" he insisted, glancing behind them. He took her arm and hurried her forward, but she yanked from his grasp and headed toward the canyon wall.

"If I climb that piñon, I can get up the cliff and look back," she called over her shoulder.

"Dammit, Dusty! They could be following us!"

"Why would they bother? We turned back." As she spoke, she unhooked her pack and dropped it into the bushes surrounding the base of the tree. "Besides, I'll be able to see them coming." Jumping to grasp the lowest branch, she pulled herself up and disappeared into the thickly needled evergreen.

His temper about to explode, Miguel squeezed his eyes shut and counted to ten, then took a deep breath and slowly let it out. Her stubbornness was endangering their lives, he fumed, taking another breath and this time counting to fifty. After repeating the exercise in patience several times, he decided he could go after her without wringing her neck and began to unfasten his pack.

"Hold it right there."

The voice was male and unfamiliar. Miguel, slowly looked around, one arm across his chest and his hand locked on the pack strap, Miguel looked around. A man stood fifty feet away, pointing a rifle at him.

"Where's your girlfriend?"

"She went ahead." To Miguel's surprise, his voice was calm.

"Without you?" The man sounded skeptical.

"We argued the whole way back here. I wanted to keep going and see the slide. She refused to come with me, then went ahead when I said I wanted to climb the cliff for a look. She doesn't like climbing. Said she wouldn't watch me break my neck."

The gunman looked from Miguel to the rock face. Miguel studied him. Closer to forty than thirty, he'd once been muscular but was now running to fat. Sunglasses and a baseball cap advertising a brand of beer rather than a sports team shaded his eyes. A cigarette hung from his lips, and his cheeks and nose were reddened with broken veins. Probably a heavy drinker who, Miguel prayed, knew less about climbing than he did.

"Let's go get her," the man said, pointing down the trail with a wave of his rifle.

"No need to arrest us," Miguel said, pretending to assume the stranger was present to enforce the warning they'd seen. "We didn't actually disobey the signs. I'll catch up with her and we'll stay away from the rock slide."

The gunman grinned mockingly. "Move along," he said.

"But officer, I don't understand. We didn't do anything wrong."

"Let's just say we need to ask your lady friend a few questions," he answered, the grin spreading into a leer. "She looks like a relative of a friend of ours. He's got a picture of her in his wallet."

Miguel cursed inwardly and fought the panic he felt preying at the edge of his mind. As he'd feared, they'd stumbled upon the kidnappers' camp and Dusty had been seen. Now the criminals wouldn't give up until they found her. How was he going to prevent them from getting their hands on her? His grip on the strap of the pack tightened as he resisted the urge to rush the man. The jagged scar that running whitely through his right cheek proved he was no stranger to violence.

And his leer made it clear he had more in mind than simply questioning Dusty. Again he barked an order for Miguel to move. Miguel obeyed, eager to put some distance between them and Dusty. He wouldn't put it past her to make a foolheardy attempt to rescue him.

"She doesn't have any relatives out here," he said over his shoulder, hoping to plant seeds of doubt in the man's mind. He heard the man's footsteps draw closer. "First time she's ever been West. Her family lives in New York. You're wasting your time."

"Shut up and keep moving."

Miguel risked a glance at him. The man had closed the distance between them, yet remained at least ten feet away. Too far away for him to try anything. His only hope was to pretend tiredness and slow his pace until the man lost patience and came close enough to be jumped.

Please, Dusty, he prayed, plodding down the trail, *leave this up to me. You could get us both killed, or at the very least, captured.*

DUSTY PEERED from between the branches, waiting until the two men passed out of sight before scrambling down from the tree and dragging her pack from the bushes. Her hands shook as she dug through its contents for Wayne's gun. Why hadn't she listened to Miguel and turned back when they first saw the sign?

Because she'd thought he was in his macho, protective mode and she'd wanted to show him how capable she was. Which was why she hadn't believed he'd seen anything, hadn't believed they were being followed.

Now his life was in danger and it was all her fault. She cursed softly, clinging to her anger to hold back the panic. Where was the damned gun?

Her fingers closed around the small box of ammunition and moments later encountered cold, comforting steel. Could she actually shoot a human being? she wondered, loading the gun with shaking hands.

Yes, she decided, if that was what it took to save Miguel. She didn't have much time, she knew; the man would expect to catch up with her fairly quickly. Leaving the pack in the bushes and stuffing the extra ammunition into her vest pocket, she began to follow their trail.

"STEP IT UP!" the man barked at Miguel as Dusty crept within hearing distance.

"This pack is heavy. I need to rest for a minute," Miguel complained. "Or do you want to carry it?" Swinging around, he shrugged out of the pack he'd unfastened, flung it and charged at the man. Dusty broke into a run as the man jumped out of the path of the pack and slammed the rifle butt into the side of Miguel's face.

Hurling herself at the gunman's back, she circled his neck with her left arm and yanked him backward, jamming her revolver against his temple, where he could see as well as feel it.

"Drop the rifle or you're a dead man!" she ordered. He obeyed, throwing the weapon to the ground. Miguel crawled after it and picked it up, then sat up unsteadily, the point of the rifle bobbing. Blood gathered on the side of his head where the blow had broken the skin.

The man lifted his hand towards the arm Dusty still had around his neck, and she pulled her stricken gaze from Miguel's injured face. "Don't even think about making a move," she said, pressing the weapon harder against the bone by his eye. His hands hovered in front of his chest and her heart beat crazily.

"Lady, you don't want to blow my head off," the man said. His hands rose another inch, but she heard a note of uncertainty in his voice.

"But I will." She forced her mind to picture the blood on Miguel's face rather than what would happen inches from her own if she pulled the trigger she now cocked.

The man's hands dropped to his sides. She wanted to sag with relief, but couldn't. Not yet.

"Get the ropes off the tent on your pack," she told Miguel instead, "and tie this sucker up." Watching him in her peripheral vision, she prayed he was capable of moving; she couldn't keep the gun trained on the stranger and tie him up at the same time. Miguel staggered as he stood, dropping the rifle and lifting both hands to his head. His eyes closed and she feared he'd lose consciousness, but his eyes opened again, then he stumbled to the pack and fell into a kneeling position beside it.

The gunman shifted his weight slightly, testing her. Did he sense her almost overwhelming need to rush to Miguel's side? She jerked him backward. "You're gonna break my spine, bitch!" he protested.

"That won't matter if I blow your head off," she snapped. The man stiffened and grew still.

Blood dripped down the side of Miguel's face as he approached them, but he carried the nylon cords from the tent. "Hands over your head," he told the gunman, "slowly."

When their captive obeyed, Dusty moved in front of him. She held the gun with both hands, determined to shoot him if necessary.

Stepping behind him, Miguel frisked him and found both a knife and a gun in his belt. "On your stomach," he ordered. Tossing the weapons aside, he tied the man's hands behind his back and ran a cord to his feet so that he could tie them, too.

When the man was completely disabled, Miguel sat down heavily, holding his head in his hands. Forgetting her own desire to collapse with relief, Dusty darted to the pack and pulled out the first-aid kit, then knelt by Miguel. Drawing his head onto her lap, she gently washed his wound with antiseptic.

"Need to question him," he protested.

"Not until the bleeding stops," she said firmly, pressing a gauze pad against the wound. The abrasions weren't deep, she saw with relief, but he winced at her touch and admitted to a bad headache. Did he have a concussion? The thought worried her, but he insisted that he hadn't lost consciousness.

"We've got to get out of here and get you to a doctor."

Miguel started to shake his head, then apparently thought better of it. "No time," he gasped. "Give me an aspirin and I'll be all right."

"You shouldn't take anything before seeing a doctor."

"Give me a damned aspirin!" He half sat up, but pain leveled him again. "If he doesn't go back to camp, his buddies will be out looking for him. With him and my head slowing us down, we'll never make it."

"What else can we do? We have to try!"

"Give me an aspirin and I'll tell you."

Dusty obeyed; if she'd listened to him in the first place and turned back, he wouldn't be hurt now.

When he'd swallowed the aspirin, Miguel insisted on questioning their captive before explaining his plan. The man tried to tell them to go to hell, but Miguel didn't waste time asking nicely. After a few well-placed kicks, the man told him his name was Sam Miller; he had two buddies named Jake Johnson and Melvin Newman in camp, a half mile beyond the sign.

"Good." Miguel grunted and sat down again. Dusty frowned, confused. "Untie his hands, one at a time," he told her. "Take his jacket off, put Wayne's on him and give him my hat and sunglasses."

"Why?"

"Just do it!" His tone was harsh and Dusty jumped to do his bidding. He held the gun on Sam while she made the change in his clothing. "I'll wear his jacket, hat and sunglasses and walk you two into camp," Miguel explained. "Put his gun in your pocket and hold

yours behind you, as though your hands were tied behind your back. I'll carry the rifle and we'll take the
other two by surprise."

"That's dangerous," Dusty objected.

"Got a better idea?"

Dusty shook her head; she felt miserable. "I'm sorry,"
she whispered, "this is all my fault. If I'd listened to you,
we could have gone for help."

"We don't have time to think about that now." His
voice was gruff and his expression unforgiving as he
donned Sam's jacket, cap and glasses. Dusty watched
him, aching for a hug, for reassurance, for a sign of his
love.

"Gag him," he ordered curtly. "We don't want him
yelling a warning when we get there."

Moving woodenly, she obeyed, but before they left,
she insisted on wetting a bandanna in the stream and
folding it into a square to put under Miguel's hat, over
the bruise darkening the side of his face. "The cold will
reduce the swelling," she explained. When she'd finished, she whispered, "I love you."

If he heard, he gave no sign. He rose to his feet and
told her to strap his backpack onto Sam and loosen his
bonds just enough to allow him to walk. As they moved
back up the trail, Dusty kept a wary eye on Miguel,
afraid he might pass out, but his wooziness seemed to
have passed.

When they reached the bushes where she'd left her
pack, he told her to wear it but to transfer the heaviest
items to Sam's. He didn't want her hampered by its full
weight when they walked into the camp.

"Move up next to Sam," he instructed her when they drew closer to the sign warning of the fictitious rock slide.

The camp, Sam had told them, was a half mile past the sign. The thieves apparently trusted their signs and remote location to keep prying eyes away. Three orange pup tents sat beside the trail, and they'd even cut down the trees that had hidden the cliff dwellings. Rope ladders led up to the crumbling entrances; faintly Dusty heard the clang of pickaxes hitting rock.

They weren't expected. A man appeared in one opening and yelled at Sam for bringing people into camp. As he scrambled down one rope ladder, two more appeared, and Dusty fought the urge to cry out when she recognized her father's blond, shaggy head.

She felt rather than saw Sam's attempt to surge forward and kicked out a foot to trip him. Burdened by the pack, he fell heavily, then frantically rubbed the side of his mouth against his shoulder, struggling to dislodge the gag.

Miguel moved up quickly, planted a foot upon his chest and pointed the rifle between his eyes. Sam stopped struggling. "Keep your hands behind your back," Miguel reminded Dusty; in the excitement she'd dropped them to her sides.

Miguel kept his head down as the other men approached, but Dusty looked up and saw recognition in her father's eyes. He didn't greet her.

He walked between the other two men, who carried guns in holsters at their sides. One of them skittered to a halt, his hand moving to his hip as his gaze flew between Miguel, and the man on the ground. Miguel swung his rifle toward the newcomer, but Sam summoned the strength to lurch upward and knock it aside. Dusty whipped her hands from behind her back and crouched, holding her revolver in both hands.

"Drop it!" she yelled.

14

DUSTY SWUNG HER PISTOL from one man to another, but everyone ignored her and erupted into action. Her father grappled with the man going for his gun. Sam rolled toward Miguel's feet, trying to trip him. The third thief turned and ran for cover.

Tightening her two-fisted grip on the .357 and bracing herself for its recoil, Dusty aimed and fired over his head. Then she rapidly shot again, lower this time so he could see the puff of dust when the bullet raked the ground beside his feet. "The next one will be in the middle of your back!" she shouted over the blasts of sound echoing off the canyon walls.

He jerked to a stop, hands over his head. Miguel staggered away from Sam, steadied his rifle and pointed it again at the big man, who fell onto his pack and lay still. Jack knocked the revolver from his opponent's grasp, slammed his fist into his jaw and sent him reeling. They both dived for the gun, but Jack came up the victor.

"On the ground, facedown, hands on your heads!" he barked. "Roll over, Sam." Burdened by the weight of the backpack, Sam flailed awkwardly and Miguel pushed him over with one foot. The other two men obeyed sullenly and Jack relieved them of their revolvers, as well as of the knives tucked inside their boots. Miguel tossed him the webbing tied on Sam's pack and Jack bound their hands, then used their shoelaces to tie their feet together.

It was over. Dusty flipped on the revolver's safety catch and dropped the suddenly unbearable weight. She shrugged out of her pack and let her shoulders slump in relief. She hadn't had to shoot anyone.

"What took you so long?" Jack asked, turning to her with a grin and holding out his arms.

A strangled sound, half sob and half chuckle escaped her and Dusty ran for the familiar haven. But halfway there, her legs seemed to turn into sponges and the ground to quicksand. She wobbled, her gaze fixed on her father's face, as she willed her muscles to complete their journey.

He strode toward her, arms still outstretched, but to her eyes he moved in a parody of slow motion. Desperate to reach him, she stumbled and pitched forward. Jack caught her, sweeping her into a bear hug. She clung to him, struck now by an uncontrollable trembling. He held her tightly, patting her back and murmuring words of love and encouragement.

Dusty barely heard him. Words spilled from her randomly as she tried to tell him of the wasted weeks of searching, of her stubborn pride that lead to Miguel's capture, of the horror of holding a gun to a human being's head and knowing she might have to pull the trigger, but she just couldn't seem to string a complete sentence together.

"One thing at a time," he interrupted gently. "Your friend looks like he's about to collapse. I think we'd better see to him."

"Sam hit him on the head with a rifle butt!" Dusty pushed herself away from her father and rushed to Miguel's side. A gray pallor tinged his dusky skin and blood reddened the bandanna covering his wound. "How do you feel?" she asked worriedly.

"Need to lie down," he mumbled and sank to the ground, head in his hands. Removing Sam's backpack with her father's help, Dusty once again dug frantically inside it for the first-aid kit.

"I'll make up a bed for him and get a fire started," Jack said. "We need to keep him warm so shock can't set in." He worked quickly and they soon had Miguel wrapped in a sleeping bag, his head pillowed in Dusty's lap. She cleaned his wound once more and Jack examined it.

"His skull doesn't appear to be fractured and since he could walk, I'd say he probably doesn't have a concussion, but . . ."

He couldn't be sure, Dusty silently finished looking at him anxiously.

"We've got to get Miguel to a doctor," she said and Jack nodded. If a blood vessel ruptured, it could take hours or days for the pressure of the leaking blood to build into recognizable symptoms of hemorrhage. He already had a headache, and at any sign of confusion, nausea, weakness, numbness or increasing drowsiness, he'd need immediate medical attention. And they faced a two-day hike back to the Willys, plus a half day's drive to reach the hospital in Moab.

"I'll set signal fires." Jack rose and began gathering wood. When he finished, three fires formed a large triangle, the symbol for help pilots of passing aircraft would recognize.

"You guys may as well do something useful for the first time in your lives," he told their captives. After checking their bonds, he ordered them to stand, then lie down again where he indicated. He spaced them well apart, and with Dusty's backpack, as well as Sam's and other items from around the camp, he formed a thirty-foot "X" across their site to alert the pilots that they also required medical attention.

Then he took the tent poles and crossed the stream to a flat, open area. Tying bright pieces of lightweight clothing to the poles, he stuck them into the ground, marking off a landing site for a helicopter.

"I can walk," Miguel protested when Jack rejoined him, but his voice was weak and his face twisted with pain when he tried to sit up.

"Stay still," Jack commanded, pushing him back down again with a hand on his chest. "No need to take any chances." He looked at Dusty's hand caressing Miguel's head, then at her face. "Especially since you've got my daughter so worried."

"It's my fault he was hurt," Dusty told him.

"We've got the time. Why don't you start at the beginning?"

Stressing how much Miguel had helped her, Dusty summarized the story of her search. Jack was pleased that Cody had survived and furious that the men had drugged or poisoned Hank. "That'll teach me to keep my big mouth shut in bars," he said when she finished, then explained how Sam had joined his farewell party at a bar in Moab before he'd left for Pinecreek. "He heard me teasing Wayne that I could save myself time and trouble if I sold all the artifacts I've found, instead of running off to Arizona looking for gold." He glowered in Sam's direction.

"The bastard was real cagey. Said he'd done some mining out in California, bought a round of drinks and wormed his way into the group. Hell, I wound up inviting him to visit me in Pinecreek and promising to give him a tour of Canyonlands when I got back in the autumn. Guess he got his friends together and decided to come and get me instead of waiting."

He paused and gave Miguel a little shake. "Keep those eyes open, boy," he said. "Don't go drifting off on us."

He cast a glance at the sky. "Damned pilots and rangers must be blind not to have spotted all this smoke by now. I'll throw some more green wood on, then we'll have to switch to dry for light, come sundown."

"Do you want some help?" Dusty asked, loath to move from Miguel's side.

"You just keep him awake." Jack moved away. Dusty bent her head and kissed Miguel on the brow. The flesh around his bandage was turning a violent purple and his eyelids fluttered shut.

"Sleepy," he murmured. "Maybe this headache would go away if I dozed."

"Fight it," Dusty urged, gripping his shoulders, but resisting the urge to shake him. "If you sleep you might slip into a coma." *And die,* she added silently. "I'm sure Wayne has his friends in the Park Service keeping an eye in this direction. Help will come soon." *Please,* she prayed.

They heard the beat of the helicopter's rotors before they saw it. It skimmed above the canyon walls, then hovered over them. Jack jumped and waved, pointing at the site he'd marked across the stream, then ran to direct the landing.

Two men with a stretcher jumped out of the copter and conferred with Jack, then crossed the stream to Dusty and Miguel. Medics as well as park rangers, they examined Miguel complimenting Dusty on her bandage. There wasn't room for her in the helicopter, they told her, loading Miguel onto the stretcher. But they'd send a larger helicopter for the rest of them.

Dusty held Miguel's hand and walked with them as they returned to the helicopter. She barely had time to kiss his cheek and tell him she'd join him soon before they lifted him inside. He made no response, and she had to back out of the way as the copter lifted off.

"At the worst he has a mild concussion," her father said, dropping an arm around her shoulders and hugging her. "And he'll be in the hospital in twenty minutes. He'll be as good as new by tomorrow."

Despite his reassurance, she couldn't summon much enthusiasm when he led her up the rope ladders to see the ruins. Timbers still framed the entrances, while crumbling walls of dry-laid stones divided the caves into separate alcoves. Standing stones formed the mealing bins, where corn had been stored. Excavations beside them revealed the *metates* and *manos* used to grind corn, arrowheads, pottery shards and frayed leather sandals. Red pictographs of wild animals and figures with broad shoulders danced across the beige sandstone walls, and blackened stone ceilings spoke of countless camp fires.

"We just started in here." Jack's voice echoed in the silent stone chambers. "We worked the trash heap down below first."

Dusty nodded, but said nothing. She knew that the humps of earth outside the dwellings, where the ancient tribes had dumped their waste, had also served as a place for burials and often rewarded both thieves and archaeologists with their richest prizes.

"We were supposed to make another delivery in two days." Jack pointed to a pile of intact pots near the entrance. "We carried them out to Salt Creek on our backs, and a man met us with a truck." He grinned. "And cold beer."

"I saw the cans."

"Picked them up?" Dusty nodded and he patted her shoulder in approval. "I think some rangers can make that rendezvous and get the guy. He can lead them to the buyers." His voice was rich with a grim satisfaction, but Dusty couldn't share it. Yes, she wanted the ring of thieves broken, but more than that, she longed to be at the hospital with Miguel. She left the caves and climbed down the ladder to wait for the helicopter's return.

Jack followed her, checked and tightened the ties on their squirming captives, put out two of the fires, then hunkered down beside her. "Are you going to marry him and give me grandchildren to rock on my knee?" he asked.

Dusty sighed, her eyes on the flickering flames. "Right now I'd say yes, but . . ."

"You didn't before, and once he's on his feet, you don't know if you will?"

Feeling miserable, but relieved she hadn't had to put her feelings into words, she nodded. "I just don't know if it will work."

"Why not?"

"If I ever married, I thought it would be to a man like me and we'd start our own business in Moab, live here all year. Miguel's very close to his family and wants to take over his mother's restaurant someday. Can you see me spending the rest of my life in Pinecreek, waiting tables in his restaurant, cleaning house and having babies?"

"I can see you doing anything you want to do."

Dusty pulled her knees to her chest and hugged them. "That's just it," she mumbled. "I want to spend my life with Miguel, but I'm afraid he wants a wife like Mom, one who's content to cook, clean and change diapers, who depends on him to make all the decisions in her life. And I couldn't bear to be tied down and cooped up. I need the wide-open spaces. We'd end up fighting all the time, like you and Mom." Her gaze rose above the fire to roam the canyon walls.

Jack was silent so long, she thought he wasn't going to respond. "Household chores can be shared, and a man can help change diapers, too," he finally said.

"And if he was willing to backpack in here after me, he'd probably share the wide-open spaces with you, too. Are you sure it's not the dependent part that scares you the most?"

Dusty lowered her head to her knees. "I hate the thought of leaving the canyons, too," she admitted. "And don't tell me it's different for a woman," she warned, raising her head to glare at him. "I love my freedom and these canyons as much as you do."

"The canyons are a good place to hide!" he said harshly, then paused and continued more calmly. "Rocks don't keep you warm at night," he pointed out, "and they don't provide much in the way of conversation, either." He dropped his gaze to the fire and spoke in such a low voice that she had to strain to hear him.

"I get lonely, Dusty. Yes, I'm free, but I'm also alone. And I have no one to blame for that but myself." He looked at her then, the lines in his weather-beaten face seeming to deepen with regret.

"I'm a coward," he added bluntly. "What I've never told you is that when Bonnie packed up, I cried like a baby and ran for the hills. I was a failure, incapable of keeping a wife or a daughter. But while I was roaming these canyons, I remembered our trips together, all the questions you used to ask and how you'd climb the rocks like a bighorn's lamb. And I knew there was something I'd given you and could still give you. And so I came back and got a lawyer and fought for summer custody."

"For that I am eternally grateful," Dusty interjected.

He ignored her. "But I've never let a woman get too close to me since. I'd failed once and I was afraid to try again. If a woman started looking serious, I lit out for the canyons again."

"It's not too late. You're still a good-looking man."

"Can't teach an old dog new tricks."

"You can if the old dog's willing."

Jack shrugged. "We're supposed to be talking about you," he grumbled. "You and Miguel are a lot older than your mother and I were. Talk to him. Tell him what you're afraid of. If he really wants a traditional wife, he wouldn't have fallen in love with a prickly canyon rat like you."

Dusty laughed as he'd intended, but he hadn't finished. "Pinecreek is hardly a city, and those mountains are full of canyons. You and Miguel can discover them together, teach your kids to love them, too. Hell, map out some good routes and offer tours, start your own business if you don't want to work in the restaurant. And you can always come back here to visit. Pinecreek isn't on the other side of the world."

He looked at her long and seriously. "You can have your cake and eat it, too, if you've both got the guts to admit you love and need one another enough to make compromises."

He sighed heavily and pulled out his tobacco pouch, his long fingers expertly rolling a cigarette. "That's where your mother and I went wrong. Like you, I was scared to death of feeling dependent on anyone. I couldn't admit that I needed her as well as loved her. Couldn't let her know how important she was to me.

For years I insisted she accept my life-style and make all
the compromises. By the time I realized I was losing her
and tried to settle down, I did too little, too late."

Lean on me, she remembered Miguel asking. Different words for admitting that she needed him. And her
father had confirmed Miguel's view of independence as
lonely, while also echoing Mamá Rosa's advice: *Remember that what you want most in the world is the
other and compromise.*

Could she relinquish her cherished self-sufficiency
and admit she needed Miguel? If she hadn't been so set
on doing things her way, she wouldn't have ignored his
advice to turn back when they saw the sign closing the
trail or stopped to climb the tree. And he wouldn't be
on his way to a hospital now. They'd be together, hiking back to the jeep to get help.

"Think about it," Jack said.

Dusty nodded and sighed. She had so much to think
about . . .

THE HELICOPTER RETURNED for them, Dusty and Jack
gave their statements to the officials and arrived at the
hospital. By that time Miguel was sleeping. X-ray had
been taken and there was no sign of fracture, his doctor assured them. They'd admitted him for the night,
since he had to be wakened every thirty minutes to
check his mental state and he'd said he had no other
option.

"He what?" Remembering she was in a hospital,
Dusty smothered her scream into an outraged whisper. Did he think she would have come back to Moab

and gone to Wayne's without checking on him? Wouldn't have cared for him? Or didn't he want her to?

"Where is he? When does he wake up next?"

The doctor's gaze slid to Jack. He was about the same age as her father, but small and portly. "Are you close relatives?" he asked.

"She's his wife," Jack lied cheerfully, "but they've had a small misunderstanding. He may not have mentioned her."

"No. He listed his mother in Arizona as next of kin on his admission form." The doctor peered at Dusty. She stared back at him, fighting the urge to snatch the chart from his fingers and learn which door separated her from the man she loved. Anger and hurt churned within her. Had Miguel decided that he no longer wanted anything to do with her?

"Please," she whispered.

The doctor checked his watch and shook his head indulgently. "Young love," he muttered to Jack, sharing a parental smile with him. "He'll probably rest better after seeing you. You can see him for five minutes young lady, but remember—" he waved an admonishing finger below her nose "—not too much excitement. The only room we had available was a private one, so you can kiss and make up, but that's it." He led them to the door of Miguel's room.

She pushed through the door, then stopped to level a warning stare at the doctor when he followed her. "I'll leave you alone," he promised. "I just want to make sure he recognizes you."

They crossed to the bed and Dusty looked at Miguel. A larger bandage had replaced hers, shockingly white against his dark hair and dusky skin. His face looked drawn and tired. His sleep didn't appear to be a restful one.

"Miguel?" Her heart seemed to rise into her throat as his eyes flickered open, eyes still shadowed with pain. But he recognized her instantly and sighed her name, reaching for her hand. She felt rather than heard the doctor leave her side.

"Wait!" she commanded, turning toward him. "He's in pain. Can't you give him something?"

The doctor shook his head. "Too risky. We've got to be certain his mind functions, and drugs will dull it." He left, swinging the door shut behind him.

"I'm checking you out of here," Dusty said firmly, turning back to Miguel. "We can stay at Wayne's and I'll wake you up every thirty minutes."

"You need your rest," Miguel objected.

"Lean on me, you said!" she retorted. "That works both ways, buster! I told you I'm no hothouse flower that has to be pampered and protected. I can set an alarm clock and survive one night's interrupted sleep. How do you expect me to learn to depend on you, if you won't depend on me?"

His eyes widened as he studied her, then he whistled softly. "Does that mean, my beautiful roadside weed, that you're going to marry me and have my babies?"

Dusty sank into the chair beside the bed and studied their entwined fingers. "Can we teach our babies to go four-wheeling and carry backpacks when they're old enough?"

"Well . . ." He hesitated and her gaze flew back to his face. "Don't you think you should teach their father first?" A glimmer of his old, teasing smile softened the lines of pain. "Let's say, starting with a nice long honeymoon backpacking in this beautiful country, minus thieves and guns?"

Dusty forgot she was in a hospital, forgot that Miguel's head ached. "Yes!" she cried and threw herself into his waiting arms.

HARLEQUIN®

Temptation®

Rebels & Rogues

Jared: He'd had the courage to fight in Vietnam. But did he have the courage to fight for the woman he loved?

THE SOLDIER OF FORTUNE
By Kelly Street
Temptation #421, December

All men are not created equal. Some are rough around the edges. Tough-minded but tenderhearted. Incredibly sexy. The tempting fulfillment of every woman's fantasy.

When it's time to fight for what they believe in, to win that special woman, our Rebels and Rogues are heroes at heart. Twelve Rebels and Rogues, one each month in 1992, only from Harlequin Temptation.

HARLEQUIN®
Temptation®

ᵗʰᵉ Fortune Boys

A funny, sexy miniseries from bestselling author Elise Title!

LOSING THEIR HEARTS MEANT LOSING THEIR FORTUNES....

If any of the four Fortune brothers were unfortunate enough to wed, they'd be permanently divorced from the Fortune millions—thanks to their father's last will and testament.

BUT CUPID HAD OTHER PLANS!
Meet Adam in #412 **ADAM & EVE** (Sept. 1992)
Meet Peter #416 **FOR THE LOVE OF PETE** (Oct. 1992)
Meet Truman in #420 **TRUE LOVE** (Nov. 1992)
Meet Taylor in #424 **TAYLOR MADE** (Dec. 1992)

WATCH THESE FOUR MEN TRY TO WIN AT LOVE AND NOT FORFEIT $$$

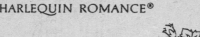

HARLEQUIN ROMANCE®

**Harlequin Romance
has love in
store for you!**

Don't miss next
month's title in

THE BRIDAL COLLECTION

A WHOLESALE ARRANGEMENT
by Day Leclaire

THE BRIDE *needed* the Groom.
THE GROOM *wanted* the Bride.
BUT THE WEDDING was *more* than
a convenient solution!

Available this month in
The Bridal Collection
Only Make-Believe
by Bethany Campbell
Harlequin Romance #3230

WELCOME TO

The quintessential small town,
where everyone knows everybody else!

Each book set in Tyler is a self-contained love story; together,
the twelve novels stitch the fabric of the community.

"The small town warmth and friendliness shine through."
Rendezvous

Join your friends in Tyler for the tenth book,
CROSSROADS by Marisa Carroll, available in December.

*Can Dr. Jeffrey Baron and nurse Cecelia Hayes discover
what's killing the residents of Worthington House?*

GREAT READING...GREAT SAVINGS...AND A
FABULOUS FREE GIFT!

With Tyler you can receive a fabulous gift, ABSOLUTELY FREE,
by collecting proofs-of-purchase found in each Tyler book.
And use our special Tyler coupons to save on your next
TYLER book purchase.

If you missed *Whirlwind* (March), *Bright Hopes* (April), *Wisconsin Wedding* (May), *Monkey Wrench* (June), *Blazing Star* (July), *Sunshine* (August), *Arrowpoint* (September), *Bachelor's Puzzle* (October) or *Milky Way* (November) and would like to order them, send your name, address, zip or postal code, along with a check or money order for $3.99 for each book ordered (please do not send cash), plus 75¢ postage and handling ($1.00 in Canada), payable to Harlequin Reader Service, to:

In the U.S.

3010 Walden Avenue
P.O. Box 1325
Buffalo, NY 14269-1325

In Canada

P.O. Box 609
Fort Erie, Ontario
L2A 5X3

Please specify book title(s) with your order.
Canadian residents add applicable federal and provincial taxes.

TYLER-10

HARLEQUIN ROMANCE®

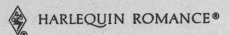

Some people have the spirit
of Christmas all year round...

People like Blake Connors
and Karin Palmer.

Meet them—and love them!—in
Eva Rutland's
ALWAYS CHRISTMAS.

Harlequin Romance #3240
Available in December wherever
Harlequin books are sold.

HRHX

HARLEQUIN ROMANCE®

After her father's heart attack, Stephanie Bloomfield comes home to Orchard Valley, Oregon, to be with him and with her sisters.

Orchard Valley

Steffie learns that many things have changed in her absence—but not her feelings for journalist Charles Tomaselli. He was the reason she left Orchard Valley. Now, three years later, will he give her a reason to stay?

"The Orchard Valley trilogy features three delightful, spirited sisters and a trio of equally fascinating men. The stories are rich with the romance, warmth of heart and humor readers expect, and invariably receive, from Debbie Macomber."

—Linda Lael Miller

Don't miss the Orchard Valley trilogy by Debbie Macomber:

VALERIE   Harlequin Romance #3232 (November 1992)
STEPHANIE   Harlequin Romance #3239 (December 1992)
NORAH   Harlequin Romance #3244 (January 1993)

Look for the special cover flash on each book!

Available wherever Harlequin books are sold.   ORC-2